IN THE CAGE

UNIFORM EDITION
OF THE TALES

IN THE CAGE

BY HENRY JAMES

LONDON: MARTIN SECKER
XVII BUCKINGHAM STREET ADELPHI

This edition first published in 1919

The text follows that of the
Definitive Edition

Date of original publication 1898

I

It had occurred to her early that in her position — that of a young person spending, in framed and wired confinement, the life of a guinea-pig or a magpie — she should know a great many persons without their recognising the acquaintance. That made it an emotion the more lively — though singularly rare and always, even then, with opportunity still very much smothered — to see any one come in whom she knew outside, as she called it, any one who could add anything to the meanness of her function. Her function was to sit there with two young men — the other telegraphist and the counter-clerk ; to mind the "sounder," which was always going, to dole out stamps and postal-orders, weigh letters, answer stupid questions, give difficult change and, more than anything else, count words as numberless as the sands of the sea, the words of the telegrams thrust, from morning to night, through the gap left in the high lattice, across the encumbered shelf that her forearm ached with rubbing. This transparent screen fenced out or fenced in, accord-

ing to the side of the narrow counter on which
the human lot was cast, the duskiest corner of a
shop pervaded not a little, in winter, by the
poison of perpetual gas, and at all times by the
presence of hams, cheese, dried fish, soap, varnish,
paraffin and other solids and fluids that she came
to know perfectly by their smells without con-
senting to know them by their names.

The barrier that divided the little post-and-
telegraph-office from the grocery was a frail
structure of wood and wire ; but the social, the
professional separation was a gulf that fortune,
by a stroke quite remarkable, had spared her the
necessity of contributing at all publicly to bridge.
When Mr. Cocker's young men stepped over from
behind the other counter to change a five-pound
note — and Mr. Cocker's situation, with the cream
of the " Court Guide " and the dearest furnished
apartments, Simpkin's, Ladle's, Thrupp's, just
round the corner, was so select that his place was
quite pervaded by the crisp rustle of these emblems
— she pushed out the sovereigns as if the applicant
were no more to her than one of the momentary,
the practically featureless, appearances in the
great procession ; and this perhaps all the more
from the very fact of the connexion (only recognised outside indeed) to which she had lent herself
with ridiculous inconsequence. She recognised

the others the less because she had at last so
unreservedly, so irredeemably, recognised Mr.
Mudge. However that might be, she was a little
ashamed of having to admit to herself that Mr.
Mudge's removal to a higher sphere — to a more
commanding position, that is, though to a much
lower neighbourhood — would have been described still better as a luxury than as the mere
simplification, the corrected awkwardness, that
she contented herself with calling it. He had at
any rate ceased to be all day long in her eyes,
and this left something a little fresh for them to
rest on of a Sunday. During the three months of
his happy survival at Cocker's after her consent
to their engagement she had often asked herself
what it was marriage would be able to add to a
familiarity that seemed already to have scraped
the platter so clean. Opposite there, behind the
counter of which his superior stature, his whiter
apron, his more clustering curls and more present,
too present, *h*'s had been for a couple of years
the principal ornament, he had moved to and fro
before her as on the small sanded floor of their
contracted future. She was conscious now of
the improvement of not having to take her
present and her future at once. They were about
as much as she could manage when taken separate.

She had, none the less, to give her mind steadily

7

to what Mr. Mudge had again written her about,
the idea of her applying for a transfer to an
office quite similar — she could n't yet hope for
a place in a bigger — under the very roof where
he was foreman, so that, dangled before her every
minute of the day, he should see her, as he called
it, " hourly," and in a part, the far N.W. district,
where, with her mother, she would save on their
two rooms alone nearly three shillings. It would
be far from dazzling to exchange Mayfair for
Chalk Farm, and it wore upon her much that he
could never drop a subject ; still, it did n't wear
as things *had* worn, the worries of the early times
of their great misery, her own, her mother's
and her elder sister's — the last of whom had
succumbed to all but absolute want when, as
conscious and incredulous ladies, suddenly bereft,
betrayed, overwhelmed, they had slipped faster
and faster down the steep slope at the bottom of
which she alone had rebounded. Her mother had
never rebounded any more at the bottom than
on the way ; had only rumbled and grumbled
down and down, making, in respect of caps,
topics and " habits," no effort whatever — which
simply meant smelling much of the time of
whiskey.

II

It was always rather quiet at Cocker's while the
contingent from Ladle's and Thrupp's and all the
other great places were at luncheon, or, as the
young men used vulgarly to say, while the animals
were feeding. She had forty minutes in advance
of this to go home for her own dinner; and
when she came back and one of the young men
took his turn there was often half an hour during
which she could pull out a bit of work or a book
— a book from the place where she borrowed
novels, very greasy, in fine print and all about
fine folks, at a ha'penny a day. This sacred
pause was one of the numerous ways in which
the establishment kept its finger on the pulse of
fashion and fell into the rhythm of the larger life.
It had something to do, one day, with the particular flare of importance of an arriving customer,
a lady whose meals were apparently irregular,
yet whom she was destined, she afterwards found,
not to forget. The girl was blasée; nothing
could belong more, as she perfectly knew, to the
intense publicity of her profession; but she had

a whimsical mind and wonderful nerves ; she was subject, in short, to sudden flickers of antipathy and sympathy, red gleams in the grey, fitful needs to notice and to " care," odd caprices of curiosity. She had a friend who had invented a new career for women — that of being in and out of people's houses to look after the flowers. Mrs. Jordan had a manner of her own of sounding this allusion ; " the flowers," on her lips, were, in fantastic places, in happy homes, as usual as the coals or the daily papers. She took charge of them, at any rate, in all the rooms, at so much a month, and people were quickly finding out what it was to make over this strange burden of the pampered to the widow of a clergyman. The widow, on her side, dilating on the initiations thus opened up to her, had been splendid to her young friend over the way she was made free of the greatest houses — the way, especially when she did the dinner-tables, set out so often for twenty, she felt that a single step more would transform her whole social position. On its being asked of her then if she circulated only in a sort of tropical solitude, with the upper servants for picturesque natives, and on her having to assent to this glance at her limitations, she had found a reply to the girl's invidious question. " You 've no imagination, my dear ! "— that was because a door more than half open to the higher life could n't be called anything but a thin partition. Mrs. Jordan's imagination quite did away with the thickness.

Our young lady had not taken up the charge, had dealt with it good-humouredly, just because she knew so well what to think of it. It was at once one of her most cherished complaints and most secret supports that people did n't understand her, and it was accordingly a matter of indifference to her that Mrs. Jordan should n't; even though Mrs. Jordan, handed down from their early twilight of gentility and also the victim of reverses, was the only member of her circle in whom she recognised an equal. She was perfectly aware that her imaginative life was the life in which she spent most of her time; and she would have been ready, had it been at all worth while, to contend that, since her outward occupation did n't kill it, it must be strong indeed. Combinations of flowers and green-stuff, forsooth! What *she* could handle freely, she said to herself, was combinations of men and women. The only weakness in her faculty came from the positive abundance of her contact with the human herd; this was so constant, it had so the effect of cheapening her privilege, that there were long stretches in which inspiration, divination and interest quite dropped. The great thing was the flashes, the quick revivals, absolute accidents all, and neither to be counted on nor to be resisted. Some one had only sometimes to put in a penny for a stamp and the whole thing was upon her. She was so absurdly constructed that these were literally the moments that made up — made up for the long stiffness of sitting there in the stocks, made up for the cunning hostility of Mr. Buckton and the importunate sympathy of the counter-clerk, made up for the daily deadly flourishy letter from Mr. Mudge, made up even for the most haunting of her worries, the rage at moments of not knowing how her mother did " get it."

She had surrendered herself moreover of late to a certain expansion of her consciousness ; something that seemed perhaps vulgarly accounted for by the fact that, as the blast of the season roared louder and the waves of fashion tossed their spray further over the counter, there were more impressions to be gathered and really — for it came to that — more life to be led. Definite at any rate was that by the time May was well started the kind of company she kept at Cocker's had begun to strike her as a reason — a reason she might almost put forward for a policy of procrastination. It sounded silly, of course, as yet, to plead such a motive, especially as the fascination of the place was after all a sort of torment. But she liked her torment ; it was a torment she should miss at Chalk Farm. She was ingenious and uncandid, therefore, about leaving the breadth of London a little longer between herself and that austerity. If she had n't quite the courage in short to say to Mr. Mudge that her actual chance for a play of mind was worth any week the three shillings he desired to help her to save, she yet saw something happen in the course of the month that in her heart of hearts at least answered the subtle question. This was connected precisely with the appearance of the memorable lady.

III

SHE pushed in three bescribbled forms which the girl's hand was quick to appropriate, Mr. Buckton having so frequent a perverse instinct for catching first any eye that promised the sort of entertainment with which she had her peculiar affinity. The amusements of captives are full of a desperate contrivance, and one of our young friend's ha'pennyworths had been the charming tale of " Picciola." It was of course the law of the place that they were never to take no notice, as Mr. Buckton said, whom they served ; but this also never prevented, certainly on the same gentleman's own part, what he was fond of describing as the underhand game. Both her companions, for that matter, made no secret of the number of favourites they had among the ladies ; sweet familiarities in spite of which she had repeatedly caught each of them in stupidities and mistakes, confusions of identity and lapses of observation that never failed to remind her how the cleverness of men ends where the cleverness of women begins. " Marguerite, Regent Street.

14

Try on at six. All Spanish lace. Pearls. The full length." That was the first ; it had no signature. " Lady Agnes Orme, Hyde Park Place. Impossible to-night, dining Haddon. Opera to-morrow, promised Fritz, but could do play Wednesday. Will try Haddon for Savoy, and anything in the world you like, if you can get Gussy. Sunday Montenero. Sit Mason Monday, Tuesday. Marguerite awful. Cissy." That was the second. The third, the girl noted when she took it, was on a foreign form : " Everard, Hôtel Brighton, Paris. Only understand and believe. 22nd to 26th, and certainly 8th and 9th. Perhaps others. Come. Mary."

Mary was very handsome, the handsomest woman, she felt in a moment, she had ever seen — or perhaps it was only Cissy. Perhaps it was both, for she had seen stranger things than that — ladies wiring to different persons under different names. She had seen all sorts of things and pieced together all sorts of mysteries. There had once been one — not long before — who, without winking, sent off five over five different signatures. Perhaps these represented five different friends who had asked her — all women, just as perhaps now Mary and Cissy, or one or other of them, were wiring by deputy. Sometimes she put in too much — too much of her own sense ;

sometimes she put in too little ; and in either
case this often came round to her afterwards,
for she had an extraordinary way of keeping
clues. When she noticed she noticed ; that was
what it came to. There were days and days,
there were weeks sometimes, of vacancy. This
arose often from Mr. Buckton's devilish and successful subterfuges for keeping her at the sounder
whenever it looked as if anything might amuse ;
the sounder, which it was equally his business to
mind, being the innermost cell of captivity, a
cage within the cage, fenced off from the rest by
a frame of ground glass. The counter-clerk
would have played into her hands ; but the
counter-clerk was really reduced to idiocy by the
effect of his passion for her. She flattered herself moreover, nobly, that with the unpleasant
conspicuity of this passion she would never have
consented to be obliged to him. The most she
would ever do would be always to shove off on
him whenever she could the registration of letters,
a job she happened particularly to loathe. After
the long stupors, at all events, there almost
always suddenly would come a sharp taste of
something ; it was in her mouth before she knew
it ; it was in her mouth now.

To Cissy, to Mary, whichever it was, she found
her curiosity going out with a rush, a mute

effusion that floated back to her, like a returning tide, the living colour and splendour of the beautiful head, the light of eyes that seemed to reflect such utterly other things than the mean things actually before them ; and, above all, the high curt consideration of a manner that even at bad moments was a magnificent habit and of the very essence of the innumerable things — her beauty, her birth, her father and mother, her cousins and all her ancestors — that its possessor couldn't have got rid of even had she wished. How did our obscure little public servant know that for the lady of the telegrams this was a bad moment ? How did she guess all sorts of impossible things, such as, almost on the very spot, the presence of drama at a critical stage and the nature of the tie with the gentleman at the Hôtel Brighton ? More than ever before it floated to her through the bars of the cage that this at last was the high reality, the bristling truth that she had hitherto only patched up and eked out — one of the creatures, in fine, in whom all the conditions for happiness actually met, and who, in the air they made, bloomed with an unwitting insolence. What came home to the girl was the way the insolence was tempered by something that was equally a part of the distinguished life, the custom of a flowerlike bend

B   17

to the less fortunate — a dropped fragrance, a mere quick breath, but which in fact pervaded and lingered. The apparition was very young, but certainly married, and our fatigued friend had a sufficient store of mythological comparison to recognise the port of Juno. Marguerite might be "awful," but she knew how to dress a goddess.

Pearls and Spanish lace — she herself, with assurance, could see them, and the "full length" too, and also red velvet bows, which, disposed on the lace in a particular manner (she could have placed them with the turn of a hand) were of course to adorn the front of a black brocade that would be like a dress in a picture. However, neither Marguerite nor Lady Agnes nor Haddon nor Fritz nor Gussy was what the wearer of this garment had really come in for. She had come in for Everard — and that was doubtless not *his* true name either. If our young lady had never taken such jumps before it was simply that she had never before been so affected. She went all the way. Mary and Cissy had been round together, in their single superb person, to see him — he must live round the corner; they had found that, in consequence of something they had come, precisely, to make up for or to have another scene about, he had gone off — gone off just on purpose to make them feel it;

18

on which they had come together to Cocker's as to the nearest place ; where they had put in the three forms partly in order not to put in the one alone. The two others in a manner, covered it, muffled it, passed it off. Oh yes, she went all the way, and this was a specimen of how she often went. She would know the hand again any time. It was as handsome and as everything else as the woman herself. The woman herself had, on learning his flight, pushed past Everard's servant and into his room ; she had written her missive at his table and with his pen. All this, every inch of it, came in the waft that she blew through and left behind her, the influence that, as I have said, lingered. And among the things the girl was sure of, happily, was that she should see her again.

IV

SHE saw her in fact, and only ten days later;
but this time not alone, and that was exactly a
part of the luck of it. Not unaware — as how
could her observation have left her so? — of the
possibilities through which it could range, our
young lady had ever since had in her mind a
dozen conflicting theories about Everard's type;
as to which, the instant they came into the place,
she felt the point settled with a thump that
seemed somehow addressed straight to her heart.
That organ literally beat faster at the approach
of the gentleman who was this time with Cissy,
and who, as seen from within the cage, became on
the spot the happiest of the happy circumstances
with which her mind had invested the friend of
Fritz and Gussy. He was a very happy circumstance indeed as, with his cigarette in his lips and
his broken familiar talk caught by his companion,
he put down the half-dozen telegrams it would
take them together several minutes to dispatch.
And here it occurred, oddly enough, that if,
shortly before, the girl's interest in his companion

had sharpened her sense for the messages then transmitted, her immediate vision of himself had the effect, while she counted his seventy words, of preventing intelligibility. *His* words were mere numbers, they told her nothing whatever; and after he had gone she was in possession of no name, of no address, of no meaning, of nothing but a vague sweet sound and an immense impression. He had been there but five minutes, he had smoked in her face, and, busy with his telegrams, with the tapping pencil and the conscious danger, the odious betrayal that would come from a mistake, she had had no wandering glances nor roundabout arts to spare. Yet she had taken him in; she knew everything; she had made up her mind.

He had come back from Paris; everything was re-arranged; the pair were again shoulder to shoulder in their high encounter with life, their large and complicated game. The fine soundless pulse of this game was in the air for our young woman while they remained in the shop. While they remained? They remained all day; their presence continued and abode with her, was in everything she did till nightfall, in the thousands of other words she counted, she transmitted, in all the stamps she detached and the letters she weighed and the change she gave, equally unconscious and unerring in each of these particulars, and not, as the run on the little office thickened with the afternoon hours, looking up at a single ugly face in the long sequence, nor really hearing the stupid questions that she patiently and perfectly answered. All patience was possible now, all questions were stupid after his, all faces were ugly. She had been sure she should see the lady again ; and even now she should perhaps, she should probably, see her often. But for him it was totally different ; she should never never see him. She wanted it too much. There was a kind of wanting that helped — she had arrived, with her rich experience, at that generalisation ; and there was another kind that was fatal. It was this time the fatal kind ; it would prevent.

Well, she saw him the very next day, and on this second occasion it was quite different ; the sense of every syllable he paid for was fiercely distinct ; she indeed felt her progressive pencil, dabbing as if with a quick caress the marks of his own, put life into every stroke. He was there a long time — had not brought his forms filled out but worked them off in a nook on the counter ; and there were other people as well — a changing pushing cluster, with every one to mind at once and endless right change to make and information to produce. But she kept hold of him throughout; she continued, for herself, in a relation with him as close as that in which, behind the hated ground glass, Mr. Buckton luckily continued with the sounder. This morning everything changed, but rather to dreariness; she had to swallow the rebuff to her theory about fatal desires, which she did without confusion and indeed with absolute levity; yet if it was now flagrant that he did live close at hand — at Park Chambers — and belonged supremely to the class that wired everything, even their expensive feelings (so that, as he never wrote, his correspondence cost him weekly pounds and pounds, and he might be in and out five times a day) there was, all the same, involved in the prospect, and by reason of its positive excess of light, a perverse melancholy, a gratuitous misery. This was at once to give it a place in an order of feelings on which I shall presently touch.

Meanwhile, for a month, he was very constant. Cissy, Mary, never re-appeared with him; he was always either alone or accompanied only by some gentleman who was lost in the blaze of his glory. There was another sense, however — and indeed there was more than one — in which she mostly found herself counting in the splendid creature with whom she had originally connected

him. He addressed this correspondent neither
as Mary nor as Cissy ; but the girl was sure of
whom it was, in Eaton Square, that he was perpetually wiring to — and all so irreproachably ! —
as Lady Bradeen.   Lady Bradeen was Cissy, Lady
Bradeen was Mary, Lady Bradeen was the friend
of Fritz and of Gussy, the customer of Marguerite, and the close ally in short (as was ideally
right, only the girl had not yet found a descrip-
tive term that was) of the most magnificent of
men.   Nothing could equal the frequency and
variety of his communications to her ladyship
but their extraordinary, their abysmal propriety.
It was just the talk — so profuse sometimes that
she wondered what was left for their real meetings — of the very happiest people.   Their real
meetings must have been constant, for half of
it was appointments and allusions, all swimming
in a sea of other allusions still, tangled in a com-
plexity of questions that gave a wondrous image
of their life.   If Lady Bradeen was Juno it was
all certainly Olympian.   If the girl, missing the
answers, her ladyship's own outpourings, vainly
reflected that Cocker's should have been one of
the bigger offices where telegrams arrived as well
as departed, there were yet ways in which, on
the whole, she pressed the romance closer by
reason of the very quantity of imagination it

24

demanded and consumed. The days and hours of this new friend, as she came to account him, were at all events unrolled, and however much more she might have known she would still have wished to go beyond. In fact she did go beyond; she went quite far enough.

But she could none the less, even after a month, scarce have told if the gentlemen who came in with him recurred or changed ; and this in spite of the fact that they too were always posting and wiring, smoking in her face and signing or not signing. The gentlemen who came in with him were nothing when he was there. They turned up alone at other times — then only perhaps with a dim richness of reference. He himself, absent as well as present, was all. He was very tall, very fair, and had, in spite of his thick preoccupations, a good-humour that was exquisite, particularly as it so often had the effect of keeping him on. He could have reached over anybody, and anybody — no matter who — would have let him ; but he was so extraordinarily kind that he quite pathetically waited, never waggling things at her out of his turn nor saying " Here ! " with horrid sharpness. He waited for pottering old ladies, for gaping slaveys, for the perpetual Buttonses from Thrupp's ; and the thing in all this that she would have liked most unspeakably to put to the test was the possibility of her having for him a personal identity that might in a particular way appeal. There were moments when he actually struck her as on her side, as arranging to help, to support, to spare her.

But such was the singular spirit of our young friend that she could remind herself with a pang that when people had awfully good manners — people of that class,— you could n't tell. These manners were for everybody, and it might be drearily unavailing for any poor particular body to be overworked and unusual. What he did take for granted was all sorts of facility ; and his high pleasantness, his relighting of cigarettes while he waited, his unconscious bestowal of opportunities, of boons, of blessings, were all a part of his splendid security, the instinct that told him there was nothing such an existence as his could ever lose by. He was somehow all at once very bright and very grave, very young and immensely complete ; and whatever he was at any moment it was always as much as all the rest the mere bloom of his beatitude. He was sometimes Everard, as he had been at the Hôtel Brighton, and he was sometimes Captain Everard. He was sometimes Philip with his surname and sometimes Philip without it. In some directions

he was merely Phil, in others he was merely
Captain. There were relations in which he was
none of these things, but a quite different person
— " the Count." There were several friends for
whom he was William. There were several for
whom, in allusion perhaps to his complexion, he
was " the Pink 'Un." Once, once only by good
luck, he had, coinciding comically, quite miracu-
lously, with another person also near to her, been
" Mudge." Yes, whatever he was, it was a part
of his happiness — whatever he was and probably
whatever he was n't. And his happiness was a
part — it became so little by little — of something
that, almost from the first of her being at Cocker's,
had been deeply with the girl.

THIS was neither more nor less than the queer extension of her experience, the double life that, in the cage, she grew at last to lead. As the weeks went on there she lived more and more into the world of whiffs and glimpses, she found her divinations work faster and stretch further. It was a prodigious view as the pressure heightened, a panorama fed with facts and figures, flushed with a torrent of colour and accompanied with wondrous world-music. What it mainly came to at this period was a picture of how London could amuse itself; and that, with the running commentary of a witness so exclusively a witness, turned for the most part to a hardening of the heart. The nose of this observer was brushed by the bouquet, yet she could never really pluck even a daisy. What could still remain fresh in her daily grind was the immense disparity, the difference and contrast, from class to class, of every instant and every motion. There were times when all the wires in the country seemed to start from the little hole-and-corner where she plied for a livelihood, and where, in the shuffle of feet, the flutter of " forms," the straying of stamps and the ring of change over the counter, the people she had fallen into the habit of remembering and fitting together with others, and of having her theories and interpretations of, kept up before her their long procession and rotation. What twisted the knife in her vitals was the way the profligate rich scattered about them, in extravagant chatter over their extravagant pleasures and sins, an amount of money that would have held the stricken household of her frightened childhood, her poor pinched mother and tormented father and lost brother and starved sister, together for a lifetime. During her first weeks she had often gasped at the sums people were willing to pay for the stuff they transmitted — the " much love " s, the " awful " regrets, the compliments and wonderments and vain vague gestures that cost the price of a new pair of boots. She had had a way then of glancing at the people's faces, but she had early learnt that if you became a telegraphist you soon ceased to be astonished. Her eye for types amounted nevertheless to genius, and there were those she liked and those she hated, her feeling for the latter of which grew to a positive possession, an instinct of observation and detection. There were the brazen women, as she called them, of the higher and the lower fashion, whose squanderings and graspings, whose struggles and secrets and love-affairs and lies, she tracked and stored up against them till she had at moments, in private, a triumphant vicious feeling of mastery and ease, a sense of carrying their silly guilty secrets in her pocket, her small retentive brain, and thereby knowing so much more about them than they suspected or would care to think. There were those she would have liked to betray, to trip up, to bring down with words altered and fatal; and all through a personal hostility provoked by the lightest signs, by their accidents of tone and manner, by the particular kind of relation she always happened instantly to feel.

There were impulses of various kinds, alternately soft and severe, to which she was constitutionally accessible and which were determined by the smallest accidents. She was rigid in general on the article of making the public itself affix its stamps, and found a special enjoyment in dealing to that end with some of the ladies who were too grand to touch them. She had thus a play of refinement and subtlety greater, she flattered herself, than any of which

she could be made the subject ; and though most
people were too stupid to be conscious of this
it brought her endless small consolations and
revenges. She recognised quite as much those
of her sex whom she would have liked to help,
to warn, to rescue, to see more of ; and that
alternative as well operated exactly through the
hazard of personal sympathy, her vision for silver
threads and moonbeams and her gift for keeping
the clues and finding her way in the tangle.
The moonbeams and silver threads presented at
moments all the vision of what poor *she* might
have made of happiness. Blurred and blank as
the whole thing often inevitably, or mercifully,
became, she could still, through crevices and
crannies, be stupefied, especially by what, in
spite of all seasoning, touched the sorest place
in her consciousness, the revelation of the golden
shower flying about without a gleam of gold for
herself. It remained prodigious to the end, the
money her fine friends were able to spend to get
still more, or even to complain to fine friends
of their own that they were in want. The
pleasures they proposed were equalled only by
those they declined, and they made their
appointments often so expensively that she was
left wondering at the nature of the delights to
which the mere approaches were so paved with

31

shillings. She quivered on occasion into the
perception of this and that one whom she
would on the chance have just simply liked to
be. Her conceit, her baffled vanity, was possibly
monstrous ; she certainly often threw herself
into a defiant conviction that she would have
done the whole thing much better. But her
greatest comfort, mostly, was her comparative
vision of the men ; by whom I mean the unmis-
takeable gentlemen, for she had no interest in the
spurious or the shabby and no mercy at all for
the poor. She could have found a sixpence,
outside, for an appearance of want ; but her
fancy, in some directions so alert, had never a
throb of response for any sign of the sordid. The
men she did track, moreover, she tracked mainly
in one relation, the relation as to which the cage
convinced her, she believed, more than anything else could have done, that it was quite the
most diffused.

She found her ladies, in short, almost always
in communication with her gentlemen, and her
gentlemen with her ladies, and she read into
the immensity of their intercourse stories and
meanings without end. Incontestably she grew
to think that the men cut the best figure ;
and in this particular, as in many others, she
arrived at a philosophy of her own, all made up

of her private notations and cynicisms. It was
a striking part of the business, for example,
that it was much more the women, on the whole,
who were after the men than the men who were
after the women : it was literally visible that the
general attitude of the one sex was that of the
object pursued and defensive, apologetic and
attenuating, while the light of her own nature
helped her more or less to conclude as to the
attitude of the other. Perhaps she herself a
little even fell into the custom of pursuit in
occasionally deviating only for gentlemen from
her high rigour about the stamps. She had
early in the day made up her mind, in fine, that
they had the best manners ; and if there were
none of them she noticed when Captain Everard
was there, there were plenty she could place
and trace and name at other times, plenty who,
with their way of being " nice " to her, and of
handling, as if their pockets were private tills
loose mixed masses of silver and gold, were such
pleasant appearances that she could envy them
without dislike. *They* never had to give change
— they only had to get it. They ranged through
every suggestion, every shade of fortune, which
evidently included indeed lots of bad luck as
well as of good, declining even toward Mr.
Mudge and his bland firm thrift, and ascending,

in wild signals and rocket-flights, almost to
within hail of her highest standard. So from
month to month she went on with them all,
through a thousand ups and downs and a thousand pangs and indifferences. What virtually
happened was that in the shuffling herd that
passed before her by far the greater part only
passed — a proportion but just appreciable
stayed. Most of the elements swam straight
away, lost themselves in the bottomless common,
and by so doing really kept the page clear. On
the clearness therefore what she did retain stood
sharply out ; she nipped and caught it, turned
it over and interwove it.

VI

SHE met Mrs. Jordan when she could, and learned from her more and more how the great people, under her gentle shake and after going through everything with the mere shops, were waking up to the gain of putting into the hands of a person of real refinement the question that the shop-people spoke of so vulgarly as that of the floral decorations. The regular dealers in these decorations were all very well; but there was a peculiar magic in the play of taste of a lady who had only to remember, through whatever intervening dusk, all her own little tables, little bowls and little jars and little other arrangements, and the wonderful thing she had made of the garden of the vicarage. This small domain, which her young friend had never seen, bloomed in Mrs. Jordan's discourse like a new Eden, and she converted the past into a bank of violets by the tone in which she said " Of course you always knew my one passion ! " She obviously met now, at any rate, a big contemporary need, measured what it was rapidly

35

becoming for people to feel they could trust her without a tremor. It brought them a peace that — during the quarter of an hour before dinner in especial — was worth more to them than mere payment could express. Mere payment, none the less, was tolerably prompt; she engaged by the month, taking over the whole thing; and there was an evening on which, in respect to our heroine, she at last returned to the charge. " It 's growing and growing, and I see that I must really divide the work. One wants an associate — of one's own kind, don't you know? You know the look they want it all to have? — of having come, not from a florist, but from one of themselves. Well, I 'm sure *you* could give it — because you *are* one. Then we *should* win. Therefore just come in with me."

" And leave the P.O. ? "

" Let the P.O. simply bring you your letters. It would bring you lots, you 'd see : orders, after a bit, by the score." It was on this, in due course, that the great advantage again came up : " One seems to live again with one's own people." It had taken some little time (after their having parted company in the tempest of their troubles and then, in the glimmering dawn, finally sighted each other again) for each to admit that the other was, in her private circle, her only equal :

but the admission came, when it did come, with
an honest groan; and since equality *was* named,
each found much personal profit in exaggerating
the other's original grandeur. Mrs. Jordan was
ten years the older, but her young friend was
struck with the smaller difference this now made :
it had counted otherwise at the time when, much
more as a friend of her mother's, the bereaved
lady, without a penny of provision and with
stopgaps, like their own, all gone, had, across
the sordid landing on which the opposite doors
of the pair of scared miseries opened and to
which they were bewilderedly bolted, borrowed
coals and umbrellas that were repaid in potatoes
and postage-stamps. It had been a questionable
help, at that time, to ladies submerged, flounder-
ing, panting, swimming for their lives, that they
were ladies ; but such an advantage could come
up again in proportion as others vanished, and
it had grown very great by the time it was the
only ghost of one they possessed. They had
literally watched it take to itself a portion of the
substance of each that had departed ; and it
became prodigious now, when they could talk
of it together, when they could look back at it
across a desert of accepted derogation, and when,
above all, they could together work up a credulity
about it that neither could otherwise work up.

Nothing was really so marked as that they felt the need to cultivate this legend much more after having found their feet and stayed their stomachs in the ultimate obscure than they had done in the upper air of mere frequent shocks. The thing they could now oftenest say to each other was that they knew what they meant; and the sentiment with which, all round, they knew it was known had well-nigh amounted to a promise not again to fall apart.

Mrs. Jordan was at present fairly dazzling on the subject of the way that, in the practice of her fairy art, as she called it, she more than peeped in — she penetrated. There was not a house of the great kind — and it was of course only a question of those, real homes of luxury — in which she was not, at the rate such people now had things, all over the place. The girl felt before the picture the cold breath of disinheritance as much as she had ever felt it in the cage; she knew moreover how much she betrayed this, for the experience of poverty had begun, in her life, too early, and her ignorance of the requirements of homes of luxury had grown, with other active knowledge, a depth of simplification. She had accordingly at first often found that in these colloquies she could only pretend she understood. Educated as she had rapidly been by her chances at Cocker's, there were still strange gaps in her learning — she could never, like Mrs. Jordan, have found her way about one of the "homes." Little by little, however, she had caught on, above all in the light of what Mrs. Jordan's redemption had materially made of that lady, giving her, though the years and the struggles had naturally not straightened a feature, an almost super-eminent air. There were women in and out of Cocker's who were quite nice and who yet did n't look well ; whereas Mrs. Jordan looked well and yet, with her extraordinarily protrusive teeth, was by no means quite nice. It would seem, mystifyingly, that it might really come from all the greatness she could live with. It was fine to hear her talk so often of dinners of twenty and of her doing, as she said, exactly as she liked with them. She spoke as if, for that matter, she invited the company. "They simply *give* me the table — all the rest, all the other effects, come afterwards."

VII

" THEN you *do* see them ? " the girl again asked.

Mrs. Jordan hesitated, and indeed the point had been ambiguous before. " Do you mean the guests ? "

Her young friend, cautious about an undue exposure of innocence, was not quite sure. " Well — the people who live there."

" Lady Ventnor ? Mrs. Bubb ? Lord Rye ? Dear, yes. Why they *like* one."

" But does one personally *know* them ? " our young lady went on, since that was the way to speak. " I mean socially, don't you know ? — as you know *me*."

" They 're not so nice as you ! " Mrs. Jordan charmingly cried. " But I *shall* see more and more of them."

Ah this was the old story. " But how soon ? "

" Why almost any day. Of course," Mrs. Jordan honestly added, " they 're nearly always out."

" Then why do they want flowers all over ? "

" Oh that does n't make any difference." Mrs. Jordan was not philosophic ; she was just evidently determined it *should n't* make any. " They 're awfully interested in my ideas, and it 's inevitable they should meet me over them."

Her interlocutress was sturdy enough. "What do you call your ideas ? "

Mrs. Jordan's reply was fine. " If you were to see me some day with a thousand tulips you 'd discover."

" A thousand ? " — the girl gaped at such a revelation of the scale of it ; she felt for the instant fairly planted out. " Well, but if in fact they never do meet you ? " she none the less pessimistically insisted.

" Never ? They *often* do — and evidently quite on purpose. We have grand long talks."

There was something in our young lady that could still stay her from asking for a personal description of these apparitions ; that showed too starved a state. But while she considered she took in afresh the whole of the clergyman's widow. Mrs. Jordan could n't help her teeth, and her sleeves were a distinct rise in the world. A thousand tulips at a shilling clearly took one further than a thousand words at a penny ; and the betrothed of Mr. Mudge, in whom the sense of the race for life was always acute, found herself wondering, with a twinge of her easy jealousy, if it might n't after all then, for *her*

also, be better — better than where she was —
to follow some such scent. Where she was was
where Mr. Buckton's elbow could freely enter
her right side and the counter-clerk's breathing
— he had something the matter with his nose —
pervade her left ear. It was something to fill
an office under Government, and she knew but
too well there were places commoner still than
Cocker's ; but it needed no great range of taste
to bring home to her the picture of servitude and
promiscuity she could n't but offer to the eye
of comparative freedom. She was so boxed up
with her young men, and anything like a margin
so absent, that it needed more art than she
should ever possess to pretend in the least to
compass, with any one in the nature of an
acquaintance — say with Mrs. Jordan herself,
flying in, as it might happen, to wire sympathetically to Mrs. Bubb — an approach to a
relation of elegant privacy. She remembered
the day when Mrs. Jordan *had*, in fact, by the
greatest chance, come in with fifty-three words
for Lord Rye and a five-pound note to change.
This had been the dramatic manner of their reunion — their mutual recognition was so great an
event. The girl could at first only see her from
the waist up, besides making but little of her
long telegram to his lordship. It was a strange

whirligig that had converted the clergyman's widow into such a specimen of the class that went beyond the sixpence.

Nothing of the occasion, all the more, had ever become dim ; least of all the way that, as her recovered friend looked up from counting, Mrs. Jordan had just blown, in explanation, through her teeth and through the bars of the cage : "I *do* flowers, you know." Our young woman had always, with her little finger crooked out, a pretty movement for counting ; and she had not forgotten the small secret advantage, a sharpness of triumph it might even have been called, that fell upon her at this moment and avenged her for the incoherence of the message, an unintelligible enumeration of numbers, colours, days, hours. The correspondence of people she did n't know was one thing ; but the correspondence of people she did had an aspect of its own for her even when she could n't understand it. The speech in which Mrs. Jordan had defined a position and announced a profession was like a tinkle of bluebells ; but for herself her one idea about flowers was that people had them at funerals, and her present sole gleam of light was that lords probably had them most. When she watched, a minute later, through the cage, the swing of her visitor's departing petticoats, she saw the sight from the waist down; and when the counter-clerk, after a mere male glance, remarked, with an intention unmistake-ably low, "Handsome woman!" she had for him the finest of her chills: "She's the widow of a bishop." She always felt, with the counter-clerk, that it was impossible sufficiently to put it on; for what she wished to express to him was the maximum of her contempt, and that element in her nature was confusedly stored. "A bishop" *was* putting it on, but the counter-clerk's approaches were vile. The night, after this, when, in the fulness of time, Mrs. Jordan mentioned the grand long talks, the girl at last brought out: "Should *I* see them? — I mean if I *were* to give up everything for you."

Mrs. Jordan at this became most arch. "I'd send you to all the bachelors!"

Our young lady could be reminded by such a remark that she usually struck her friend as pretty. "Do *they* have their flowers?"

"Oceans. And they're the most particular." Oh it was a wonderful world. "You should see Lord Rye's."

"His flowers?"

"Yes, and his letters. He writes me pages on pages — with the most adorable little drawings and plans. You should see his diagrams!"

VIII

THE girl had in course of time every opportunity to inspect these documents, and they a little disappointed her ; but in the mean while there had been more talk, and it had led to her saying, as if her friend's guarantee of a life of elegance were not quite definite : " Well, I see every one at *my* place."

" Every one ? "

" Lots of swells. They flock. They live, you know, all round, and the place is filled with all the smart people, all the fast people, those whose names are in the papers — mamma has still The Morning Post — and who come up for the season."

Mrs. Jordan took this in with complete intelligence. " Yes, and I dare say it 's some of your people that *I* do."

Her companion assented, but discriminated. " I doubt if you ' do ' them as much as I ! Their affairs, their appointments and arrangements, their little games and secrets and vices — those things all pass before me."

45

This was a picture that could make a clergyman's widow not imperceptibly gasp ; it was in intention moreover something of a retort to the thousand tulips. " Their vices ? Have they got vices ? "

Our young critic even more overtly stared ; then with a touch of contempt in her amusement : " Have n't you found *that* out ? " The homes of luxury then had n't so much to give. " *I* find out everything."

Mrs. Jordan, at bottom a very meek person, was visibly struck. " I see. You do ' have ' them."

" Oh I don't care ! Much good it. does me ! "

Mrs. Jordan after an instant recovered her superiority. " No — it does n't lead to much." Her own initiations so clearly did. Still — after all ; and she was not jealous : " There must be a charm."

" In seeing them ? " At this the girl suddenly let herself go. " I hate them. There 's that charm ! "

Mrs. Jordan gaped again. " The *real* ' smarts ' ? "

" Is that what you call Mrs. Bubb ? Yes — it comes to me ; I 've had Mrs. Bubb. I don't think she has been in herself, but there are things her maid has brought. Well, my dear ! " — and

IN THE CAGE

the young person from Cocker's, recalling these things and summing them up, seemed suddenly to have much to say. She did n't say it, however; she checked it; she only brought out: " Her maid, who 's horrid — *she* must have her ! " Then she went on with indifference : " They 're *too* real ! They 're selfish brutes."

Mrs. Jordan, turning it over, adopted at last the plan of treating it with a smile. She wished to be liberal. " Well, of course, they do lay it out."

" They bore me to death," her companion pursued with slightly more temperance.

But this was going too far. " Ah that's because you 've no sympathy ! "

The girl gave an ironic laugh, only retorting that nobody could have any who had to count all day all the words in the dictionary ; a contention Mrs. Jordan quite granted, the more that she shuddered at the notion of ever failing of the very gift to which she owed the vogue — the rage she might call it — that had caught her up. Without sympathy — or without imagination, for it came back again to that — how should she get, for big dinners, down the middle and toward the far corners at all ? It was n't the combinations, which were easily managed : the strain was over the ineffable simplicities, those

47

that the bachelors above all, and Lord Rye perhaps most of any, threw off — just blew off like cigarette-puffs — such sketches of. The betrothed of Mr. Mudge at all events accepted the explanation, which had the effect, as almost any turn of their talk was now apt to have, of bringing her round to the terrific question of that gentleman. She was tormented with the desire to get out of Mrs. Jordan, on this subject, what she was sure was at the back of Mrs. Jordan's head ; and to get it out of her, queerly enough, if only to vent a certain irritation at it. She knew that what her friend would already have risked if she had n't been timid and tortuous was : " Give him up — yes, give him up : you 'll see that with your sure chances you 'll be able to do much better."

Our young woman had a sense that if that view could only be put before her with a particular sniff for poor Mr. Mudge she should hate it as much as she morally ought. She was conscious of not, as yet, hating it quite so much as that. But she saw that Mrs. Jordan was conscious of something too, and that there was a degree of confidence she was waiting little by little to arrive at. The day came when the girl caught a glimpse of what was still wanting to make her friend feel strong ; which was nothing less than the prospect of being able to announce the climax of sundry private dreams. The associate of the aristocracy had personal calculations — matter for brooding and dreaming, even for peeping out not quite hopelessly from behind the window-curtains of lonely lodgings. If she did the flowers for the bachelors, in short, did n't she expect that to have consequences very different from such an outlook at Cocker's as she had pronounced wholly desperate ? There seemed in very truth something auspicious in the mixture of bachelors and flowers, though, when looked hard in the eye, Mrs. Jordan was not quite prepared to say she had expected a positive proposal from Lord Rye to pop out of it. Our young woman arrived at last, none the less, at a definite vision of what was in her mind. This was a vivid foreknowledge that the betrothed of Mr. Mudge would, unless conciliated in advance by a successful rescue, almost hate her on the day she should break a particular piece of news. How could that unfortunate otherwise endure to hear of what, under the protection of Lady Ventnor, was after all so possible ?

IX

MEANWHILE, since irritation sometimes relieved her, the betrothed of Mr. Mudge found herself indebted to that admirer for amounts of it perfectly proportioned to her fidelity. She always walked with him on Sundays, usually in the Regent's Park, and quite often, once or twice a month he took her, in the Strand or thereabouts, to see a piece that was having a run. The productions he always preferred were the really good ones — Shakespeare , Thompson or some funny American thing ; which, as it also happened that she hated vulgar plays, gave him ground for what was almost the fondest of his approaches, the theory that their tastes were, blissfully, just the same. He was for ever reminding her of that, rejoicing over it and being affectionate and wise about it. There were times when she wondered how in the world she could " put up with " him, how she could put up with any man so smugly unconscious of the immensity of her difference. It was just for this difference that, if she was to be liked at all, she wanted to be liked, and if that was not the
50

source of Mr. Mudge's admiration, she asked herself what on earth *could* be ? She was not different only at one point, she was different all round ; unless perhaps indeed in being practically human, which her mind just barely recognised that he also was. She would have made tremendous concessions in other quarters : there was no limit for instance to those she would have made to Captain Everard ; but what I have named was the most she was prepared to do for Mr. Mudge. It was because *he* was different that, in the oddest way, she liked as well as deplored him ; which was after all a proof that the disparity, should they frankly recognise it, would n't necessarily be fatal. She felt that, oleaginous — too oleaginous — as he was, he was somehow comparatively primitive : she had once, during the portion of his time at Cocker's that had overlapped her own, seen him collar a drunken soldier, a big violent man who, having come in with a mate to get a postal-order cashed, had made a grab at the money before his friend could reach it and had so determined, among the hams and cheeses and the lodgers from Thrupp's, immediate and alarming reprisals, a scene of scandal and consternation. Mr. Buckton and the counter-clerk had crouched within the cage, but Mr. Mudge had, with a very quiet but very quick step round the counter, an air of masterful authority she should n't soon forget, triumphantly interposed in the scrimmage, parted the combatants and shaken the delinquent in his skin. She had been proud of him at that moment, and had felt that if their affair had not already been settled the neatness of his execution would have left her without resistance.

Their affair had been settled by other things : by the evident sincerity of his passion and by the sense that his high white apron resembled a front of many floors. It had gone a great way with her that he would build up a business to his chin, which he carried quite in the air. This could only be a question of time ; he would have all Piccadilly in the pen behind his ear. That was a merit in itself for a girl who had known what she had known. There were hours at which she even found him good-looking, though, frankly there could be no crown for her effort to imagine on the part of the tailor or the barber some such treatment of his appearance as would make him resemble even remotely a man of the world. His very beauty was the beauty of a grocer, and the finest future would offer it none too much room consistently to develop. She had engaged herself in short to the perfection of a type, and almost anything square and smooth and whole had its weight for a person still conscious herself of being a mere bruised fragment of wreckage. But it contributed hugely at present to carry on the two parallel lines of her experience in the cage and her experience out of it. After keeping quiet for some time about this opposition she suddenly — one Sunday afternoon on a penny chair in the Regent's Park — broke, for him, capriciously, bewilderingly, into an intimation of what it came to. He had naturally pressed more and more on the point of her again placing herself where he could see her hourly, and for her to recognise that she had as yet given him no sane reason for delay he had small need to describe himself as unable to make out what she was up to. As if, with her absurd bad reasons, she could have begun to tell him ! Sometimes she thought it would be amusing to let him have them full in the face, for she felt she should die of him unless she once in a while stupefied him ; and sometimes she thought it would be disgusting and perhaps even fatal. She liked him, however, to think her silly, for that gave her the margin which at the best she would always require ; and the only difficulty about this was that he hadn't enough imagination to oblige her. It produced none the less something of the desired effect — to leave him simply wondering why, over the matter of their reunion, she didn't yield to his arguments. Then at last, simply as

if by accident and out of mere boredom on a day
that was rather flat, she preposterously produced
her own. "Well, wait a bit. Where I am I
still see things." And she talked to him even
worse, if possible, than she had talked to Mrs.
Jordan.

Little by little, to her own stupefaction, she
caught that he was trying to take it as she meant
it and that he was neither astonished nor angry.
Oh the British tradesman — this gave her an idea
of his resources ! Mr. Mudge would be angry
only with a person who, like the drunken soldier
in the shop, should have an unfavourable effect
on business. He seemed positively to enter,
for the time and without the faintest flash of
irony or ripple of laughter, into the whimsical
grounds of her enjoyment of Cocker's custom,
and instantly to be casting up whatever it might,
as Mrs. Jordan had said, lead to. What he had
in mind was not of course what Mrs. Jordan had
had : it was obviously not a source of speculation
with him that his sweetheart might pick up a
husband. She could see perfectly that this was
not for a moment even what he supposed she
herself dreamed of. What she had done was
simply to give his sensibility another push into the
dim vast of trade. In that direction it was all
alert, and she had whisked before it the mild

fragrance of a " connexion." That was the most he could see in any account of her keeping in, on whatever roundabout lines, with the gentry ; and when, getting to the bottom of this, she quickly proceeded to show him the kind of eye she turned on such people and to give him a sketch of what that eye discovered, she reduced him to the particular prostration in which he could still be amusing to her.

X

"THEY'RE the most awful wretches, I assure you — the lot all about there."

"Then why do you want to stay among them?"

"My dear man, just because they *are*. It makes me hate them so."

"Hate them? I thought you liked them."

"Don't be stupid. What I 'like' is just to loathe them. You would n't believe what passes before my eyes."

"Then why have you never told me? You did n't mention anything before I left."

"Oh I had n't got round to it then. It 's the sort of thing you don't believe at first; you have to look round you a bit and then you understand. You work into it more and more. Besides," the girl went on, "this is the time of the year when the worst lot come up. They 're simply packed together in those smart streets. Talk of the numbers of the poor! What *I* can vouch for is the numbers of the rich! There are new ones every day, and they seem to get richer and richer. Oh, they do come up!" she cried, imitating for her private recreation — she was sure it would n't reach Mr. Mudge — the low intonation of the counter-clerk.

" And where do they come from ? " her companion candidly enquired.

She had to think a moment ; then she found something. " From the ' spring meetings.' They bet tremendously."

" Well, they bet enough at Chalk Farm, if that 's all."

" It *is n't* all. It is n't a millionth part ! " she replied with some sharpness. " It 's immense fun " — she *had* to tantalise him. Then as she had heard Mrs. Jordan say, and as the ladies at Cocker's even sometimes wired, " It 's quite too dreadful ! " She could fully feel how it was Mr. Mudge's propriety, which was extreme — he had a horror of coarseness and attended a Wesleyan chapel — that prevented his asking for details. But she gave him some of the more innocuous in spite of himself, especially putting before him how, at Simpkin's and Ladle's, they all made the money fly. That was indeed what he liked to hear : the connexion was not direct, but one was somehow more in the right place where the money was flying than where it was simply and meagrely nesting. The air felt that stir, he had to acknowledge, much less at Chalk Farm than

in the district in which his beloved so oddly
enjoyed her footing. She gave him, she could
see, a restless sense that these might be familiarities not to be sacrificed ; germs, possibilities,
faint foreshowings — heaven knew what — of the
initiation it would prove profitable to have
arrived at when in the fulness of time he should
have his own shop in some such paradise. What
really touched him — that was discernible — was
that she could feed him with so much mere vivid-
ness of reminder, keep before him, as by the
play of a fan, the very wind of the swift bank-
notes and the charm of the existence of a class
that Providence had raised up to be the blessing
of grocers. He liked to think that the class was
there, that it was always there, and that she
contributed in her slight but appreciable degree
to keep it up to the mark. He could n't have
formulated his theory of the matter, but the
exuberance of the aristocracy was the advantage
of trade, and everything was knit together in a
richness of pattern that it was good to follow
with one's finger-tips. It was a comfort to him
to be thus assured that there were no symptoms
of a drop. What did the sounder, as she called
it, nimbly worked, do but keep the ball going ?

What it came to therefore for Mr. Mudge was
that all enjoyments were, as might be said, inter-

related, and that the more people had the more
they wanted to have. The more flirtations, as
he might roughly express it, the more cheese and
pickles. He had even in his own small way been
dimly struck with the linkèd sweetness connecting
the tender passion with cheap champagne, or
perhaps the other way round. What he would
have liked to say had he been able to work out
his thought to the end was : " I see, I see. Lash
them up then, lead them on, keep them going :
some of it can't help, some time, coming *our* way."
Yet he was troubled by the suspicion of subtleties
on his companion's part that spoiled the straight
view. He couldn't understand people's hating
what they liked or liking what they hated ; above
all it hurt him somewhere — for he had his private
delicacies — to see anything *but* money made out
of his betters. To be too enquiring, or in any other
way too free, at the expense of the gentry was
vaguely wrong ; the only thing that was distinctly
right was to be prosperous at any price. Was n't it
just because they were up there aloft that they were
lucrative ? He concluded at any rate by saying
to his young friend : " If it 's improper for you to
remain at Cocker's, then that falls in exactly with
the other reasons I 've put before you for your
removal."

" Improper ? " — her smile became a prolonged

boldness. "My dear boy, there's no one like you!"

"I dare say," he laughed; "but that does n't help the question."

"Well," she returned, "I can't give up my friends. I'm making even more than Mrs. Jordan."

Mr. Mudge considered. "How much is *she* making?"

"Oh you dear donkey!"—and, regardless of all the Regent's Park, she patted his cheek. This was the sort of moment at which she was absolutely tempted to tell him that she liked to be near Park Chambers. There was a fascination in the idea of seeing if, on a mention of Captain Everard, he would n't do what she thought he might; would n't weigh against the obvious objection the still more obvious advantage. The advantage of course could only strike him at the best as rather fantastic; but it was always to the good to keep hold when you *had* hold, and such an attitude would also after all involve a high tribute to her fidelity. Of one thing she absolutely never doubted: Mr. Mudge believed in her with a belief——! She believed in herself too, for that matter: if there was a thing in the world no one could charge her with it was being the kind of low barmaid person who rinsed tumblers and bandied slang. But she forbore as yet to speak ; she had not spoken even to Mrs. Jordan ; and the hush that on her lips surrounded the Captain's name maintained itself as a kind of symbol of the success that, up to this time, had attended something or other — she could n't have said what — that she humoured herself with calling, without words, her relation with him.

XI

She would have admitted indeed that it consisted of little more than the fact that his absences, however frequent and however long, always ended with his turning up again. It was nobody's business in the world but her own if that fact continued to be enough for her. It was of course not enough just in itself; what it had taken on to make it so was the extraordinary possession of the elements of his life that memory and attention had at last given her. There came a day when this possession on the girl's part actually seemed to enjoy between them, while their eyes met, a tacit recognition that was half a joke and half a deep solemnity. He bade her good morning always now; he often quite raised his hat to her. He passed a remark when there was time or room, and once she went so far as to say to him that she had n't seen him for " ages." " Ages " was the word she consciously and carefully, though a trifle tremulously, used ; " ages " was exactly what she meant. To this he replied in terms doubtless less anxiously selected, but perhaps on that account not the less remarkable, " Oh yes, has n't it been awfully wet ? " That was a specimen of their give and take ; it fed her fancy that no form of intercourse so transcendent and distilled had ever been established on earth. Everything, so far as they chose to consider it so, might mean almost anything. The want of margin in the cage, when he peeped through the bars, wholly ceased to be appreciable. It was a drawback only in superficial commerce. With Captain Everard she had simply the margin of the universe. It may be imagined therefore how their unuttered reference to all she knew about him could in this immensity play at its ease. Every time he handed in a telegram it was an addition to her knowledge : what did his con-stant smile mean to mark if it did n't mean to mark that ? He never came into the place with-out saying to her in this manner : " Oh yes, you have me by this time so completely at your mercy that it does n't in the least matter what I give you now. You 've become a comfort, I assure you ! "

She had only two torments ; the greatest of which was that she could n't, not even once or twice, touch with him on some individual fact. She would have given anything to have been able to allude to one of his friends by name, to one of his engagements by date, to one of his difficulties by the solution. She would have given almost as much for just the right chance — it would have to be tremendously right — to show him in some sharp sweet way that she had perfectly penetrated the greatest of these last and now lived with it in a kind of heroism of sympathy. He was in love with a woman to whom, and to any view of whom, a lady-telegraphist, and especially one who passed a life among hams and cheeses, was as the sand on the floor; and what her dreams desired was the possibility of its somehow coming to him that her own interest in him could take a pure and noble account of such an infatuation and even of such an impropriety. As yet, however, she could only rub along with the hope that an accident, sooner or later, might give her a lift toward popping out with something that would surprise and perhaps even, some fine day, assist him. What could people mean moreover — cheaply sarcastic people — by not feeling all that could be got out of the weather? *She* felt it all, and seemed literally to feel it most when she went quite wrong, speaking of the stuffy days as cold, of the cold ones as stuffy, and betraying how little she knew, in her cage, of whether it was foul or fair. It was for that matter always stuffy at Cocker's, and she finally settled

she only asked of it to reach the point of his not
going away because of her own.   He had at times
to be away for weeks ; he had to lead his life ;
he had to travel — there were places to which he
was constantly wiring for " rooms " : all this she
granted him, forgave him ; in fact, in the long
run, literally blessed and thanked him for.   If
he had to lead his life, that precisely fostered his
leading it so much by telegraph : therefore the
benediction was to come in when he could.   That
was all she asked — that he should n't wholly
deprive her.

Sometimes she almost felt that he could n't
have deprived her even had he been minded, by
reason of the web of revelation that was woven
between them.   She quite thrilled herself with
thinking what, with such a lot of material, a bad
girl would do.   It would be a scene better than
many in her ha'penny novels, this going to him
in the dusk of evening at Park Chambers and
letting him at last have it.   " I know too much
about a certain person now not to put it to you
— excuse my being so lurid — that it 's quite worth
your while to buy me off.   Come, therefore ; buy
me ! "   There was a point indeed at which such
flights had to drop again — the point of an
unreadiness to name, when it came to that, the
purchasing medium.   It would n't certainly be

anything so gross as money, and the matter accordingly remained rather vague, all the more that *she* was not a bad girl. It was n't for any such reason as might have aggravated a mere minx that she often hoped he would again bring Cissy. The difficulty of this, however, was constantly present to her, for the kind of communion to which Cocker's so richly ministered rested on the fact that Cissy and he were so often in different places. She knew by this time all the places — Suchbury, Monkhouse, Whiteroy, Finches — and even how the parties on these occasions were composed ; but her subtlety found ways to make her knowledge fairly protect and promote their keeping, as she had heard Mrs. Jordan say, in touch. So, when he actually sometimes smiled as if he really felt the awkwardness of giving her again one of the same old addresses, all her being went out in the desire — which her face must have expressed — that he should recognise her forbearance to criticise as one of the finest tenderest sacrifices a woman had ever made for love.

XII

SHE was occasionally worried, however this might be, by the impression that these sacrifices, great as they were, were nothing to those that his own passion had imposed ; if indeed it was not rather the passion of his confederate, which had caught him up and was whirling him round like a great steam-wheel. He was at any rate in the strong grip of a dizzy splendid fate ; the wild wind of his life blew him straight before it. Did n't she catch in his face at times, even through his smile and his happy habit, the gleam of that pale glare with which a bewildered victim appeals, as he passes, to some pair of pitying eyes ? He perhaps did n't even himself know how scared he was ; but *she* knew. They were in danger, they were in danger, Captain Everard and Lady Bradeen : it beat every novel in the shop. She thought of Mr. Mudge and his safe sentiment ; she thought of herself and blushed even more for her tepid response to it. It was a comfort to her at such moments to feel that in another relation — a relation supplying that affinity with her nature that Mr. Mudge, deluded creature, would never supply — she should have been no more tepid than her ladyship. Her deepest soundings were on two or three occasions of finding herself almost sure that, if she dared, her ladyship's lover would have gathered relief from "speaking" to her. She literally fancied once or twice that, projected as he was toward his doom, her own eyes struck him, while the air roared in his ears, as the one pitying pair in the crowd. But how could he speak to her while she sat sandwiched there between the counter-clerk and the sounder ?

She had long ago, in her comings and goings made acquaintance with Park Chambers and reflected as she looked up at their luxurious front that *they* of course would supply the ideal setting for the ideal speech. There was not an object in London that, before the season was over, was more stamped upon her brain. She went roundabout to pass it, for it was not on the short way ; she passed on the opposite side of the street and always looked up, though it had taken her a long time to be sure of the particular set of windows. She had made that out finally by an act of audacity that at the time had almost stopped her heart-beats and that in retrospect greatly quickened her blushes. One evening she had lingered late and watched —

watched for some moment when the porter, who was in uniform and often on the steps, had gone in with a visitor. Then she followed boldly, on the calculation that he would have taken the visitor up and that the hall would be free. The hall *was* free, and the electric light played over the gilded and lettered board that showed the names and numbers of the occupants of the different floors. What she wanted looked straight at her — Captain Everard was on the third. It was as if, in the immense intimacy of this, they were, for the instant and the first time, face to face outside the cage. Alas! they were face to face but a second or two: she was whirled out on the wings of a panic fear that he might just then be entering or issuing. This fear was indeed, in her shameless deflexions, never very far from her, and was mixed in the oddest way with depressions and disappointments. It was dreadful, as she trembled by, to run the risk of looking to him as if she basely hung about; and yet it was dreadful to be obliged to pass only at such moments as put an encounter out of the question.

At the horrible hour of her first coming to Cocker's he was always — it was to be hoped — snug in bed; and at the hour of her final departure he was of course — she had such things all on her fingers'-ends — dressing for dinner. We may let it pass that if she could n't bring herself to hover till he was dressed, this was simply because such a process for such a person could only be terribly prolonged. When she went in the middle of the day to her own dinner she had too little time to do anything but go straight, though it must be added that for a real certainty she would joyously have omitted the repast. She had made up her mind as to there being on the whole no decent pretext to justify her flitting casually past at three o'clock in the morning. That was the hour at which, if the ha'penny novels were not all wrong, he probably came home for the night. She was therefore reduced to the vainest figuration of the miraculous meeting toward which a hundred impossibilities would have to conspire. But if nothing was more impossible than the fact, nothing was more intense than the vision. What may not, we can only moralise, take place in the quickened muffled perception of a young person with an ardent soul ? All our humble friend's native distinction, her refinement of personal grain, of heredity, of pride, took refuge in this small throbbing spot ; for when she was most conscious of the abjection of her vanity and the pitifulness of her little flutters and manœuvres, then the consolation and the redemption were most sure to glow before her in some just discernible sign. He did like her !

XIII

HE never brought Cissy back, but Cissy came
one day without him, as fresh as before from
the hands of Marguerite, or only, at the season's
end, a trifle less fresh. She was, however, distinctly less serene. She had brought nothing
with her and looked about with impatience for
the forms and the place to write. The latter
convenience, at Cocker's, was obscure and barely
adequate, and her clear voice had the light note
of disgust which her lover's never showed as she
responded with a " There ? " of surprise to the
gesture made by the counter-clerk in answer to
her sharp question. Our young friend was busy
with half a dozen people, but she had dispatched
them in her most businesslike manner by the time
her ladyship flung through the bars this light of
re-appearance. Then the directness with which
the girl managed to receive the accompanying
missive was the result of the concentration that
had caused her to make the stamps fly during the
few minutes occupied by the production of it.
This concentration, in turn, may be described

73

as the effect of the apprehension of imminent relief. It was nineteen days, counted and checked off, since she had seen the object of her homage; and as, had he been in London, she should, with his habits, have been sure to see him often, she was now about to learn what other spot his presence might just then happen to sanctify. For she thought of them, the other spots, as ecstatically conscious of it, expressively happy in it.

But, gracious, how handsome *was* her ladyship, and what an added price it gave him that the air of intimacy he threw out should have flowed originally from such a source! The girl looked straight through the cage at the eyes and lips that must so often have been so near his own — looked at them with a strange passion that for an instant had the result of filling out some of the gaps, supplying the missing answers, in his correspondence. Then as she made out that the features she thus scanned and associated were totally unaware of it, that they glowed only with the colour of quite other and not at all guessable thoughts, this directly added to their splendour, gave the girl the sharpest impression she had yet received of the uplifted, the unattainable plains of heaven, and yet at the same time caused her to thrill with a sense of the high company she did somehow keep. She

was with the absent through her ladyship and
with her ladyship through the absent. The only
pang — but it did n't matter — was the proof in
the admirable face, in the sightless preoccupa-
tion of its possessor, that the latter had n't a
notion of her. Her folly had gone to the point
of half believing that the other party to the
affair must sometimes mention in Eaton Square
the extraordinary little person at the place from
which he so often wired. Yet the perception of
her visitor's blankness actually helped this extraordinary little person, the next instant, to take
refuge in a reflexion that could be as proud as
it liked. "How little she knows, how little she
knows!" the girl cried to herself; for what did
that show after all but that Captain Everard's
telegraphic confidant was Captain Everard's
charming secret? Our young friend's perusal
of her ladyship's telegram was literally prolonged
by a momentary daze: what swam between her
and the words, making her see them as through
rippled shallow sunshot water, was the great,
the perpetual flood of "How much *I* know — how
much *I* know!" This produced a delay in her
catching that, on the face, these words did n't
give her what she wanted, though she was prompt
enough with her remembrance that her grasp
was, half the time, just of what was *not* on the

face. " Miss Dolman, Parade Lodge, Parade
Terrace, Dover. Let him instantly know right
one, Hôtel de France, Ostend. Make it seven
nine four nine six one. Wire me alternative
Burfield's."

The girl slowly counted. Then he was at
Ostend. This hooked on with so sharp a click
that, not to feel she was as quickly letting it all
slip from her, she had absolutely to hold it a
minute longer and to do something to that end.
Thus it was that she did on this occasion what
she never did — threw off a " Reply paid ? " that
sounded officious, but that she partly made up
for by deliberately affixing the stamps and by
waiting till she had done so to give change. She
had, for so much coolness, the strength that she
considered she knew all about Miss Dolman.

" Yes — paid." She saw all sorts of things in
this reply, even to a small suppressed start of
surprise at so correct an assumption ; even to
an attempt the next minute at a fresh air of
detachment. " How much, with the answer ? "
The calculation was not abstruse, but our intense
observer required a moment more to make it,
and this gave her ladyship time for a second
thought. " Oh just wait ! " The white be-
gemmed hand bared to write rose in sudden
nervousness to the side of the wonderful face

which, with eyes of anxiety for the paper on the counter, she brought closer to the bars of the cage. " I think I must alter a word ! " On this she recovered her telegram and looked over it again ; but she had a new, an obvious trouble, and studied it without deciding and with much of the effect of making our young woman watch her.

This personage, meanwhile, at the sight of her expression, had decided on the spot. If she had always been sure they were in danger her lady-ship's expression was the best possible sign of it. There was a word wrong, but she had lost the right one, and much clearly depended on her finding it again. The girl, therefore, sufficiently estimating the affluence of customers and the distraction of Mr. Buckton and the counter-clerk, took the jump and gave it. " Is n't it Cooper's ? "

It was as if she had bodily leaped — cleared the top of the cage and alighted on her inter-locutress. " Cooper's ? " — the stare was height-ened by a blush. Yes, she had made Juno blush.

This was all the greater reason for going on. " I mean instead of Burfield's."

Our young friend fairly pitied her ; she had made her in an instant so helpless, and yet not a bit haughty nor outraged. She was only mys-tified and scared. " Oh, you know —— ? "

"Yes, I know!" Our young friend smiled, meeting the other's eyes, and, having made Juno blush, proceeded to patronise her. "*I'll* do it" — she put out a competent hand. Her ladyship only submitted, confused and bewildered, all presence of mind quite gone; and the next moment the telegram was in the cage again and its author out of the shop. Then quickly, boldly, under all the eyes that might have witnessed her tampering, the extraordinary little person at Cocker's made the proper change. People were really too giddy, and if they *were*, in a certain case, to be caught, it shouldn't be the fault of her own grand memory. Hadn't it been settled weeks before ? — for Miss Dolman it was always to be "Cooper's."

XIV

But the summer " holidays " brought a marked
difference ; they were holidays for almost every
one but the animals in the cage. The August
days were flat and dry, and, with so little to feed
it, she was conscious of the ebb of her interest
in the secrets of the refined. She was in a
position to follow the refined to the extent of
knowing — they had made so many of their arrangements with her aid — exactly where they
were ; yet she felt quite as if the panorama had
ceased unrolling and the band stopped playing.
A stray member of the latter occasionally turned
up, but the communications that passed before
her bore now largely on rooms at hotels, prices
of furnished houses, hours of trains, dates of
sailings and arrangements for being " met " : she
found them for the most part prosaic and coarse.
The only thing was that they brought into her
stuffy corner as straight a whiff of Alpine meadows
and Scotch moors as she might hope ever to
inhale ; there were moreover in especial fat hot
dull ladies who had out with her, to exasperation,

the terms for seaside lodgings, which struck her as huge, and the matter of the number of beds required, which was not less portentous : this in reference to places of which the names — Eastbourne, Folkestone, Cromer, Scarborough, Whitby — tormented her with something of the sound of the plash of water that haunts the traveller in the desert. She had not been out of London for a dozen years, and the only thing to give a taste to the present dead weeks was the spice of a chronic resentment. The sparse customers, the people she did see, were the people who were " just off " — off on the decks of fluttered yachts, off to the uttermost point of rocky headlands where the very breeze was then playing for the want of which she said to herself that she sickened.

There was accordingly a sense in which, at such a period, the great differences of the human condition could press upon her more than ever ; a circumstance drawing fresh force in truth from the very fact of the chance that at last, for a change, did squarely meet her — the chance to be " off," for a bit, almost as far as anybody. They took their turns in the cage as they took them both in the shop and at Chalk Farm ; she had known these two months that time was to be allowed in September — no less than eleven days—for her personal private holiday. Much of her recent intercourse with Mr. Mudge had consisted of the hopes and fears, expressed mainly by himself, involved in the question of their getting the same dates — a question that, in proportion as the delight seemed assured, spread into a sea of speculation over the choice of where and how. All through July, on the Sunday evenings and at such other odd times as he could seize, he had flooded their talk with wild waves of calculation. It was practically settled that, with her mother, somewhere " on the south coast " (a phrase of which she liked the sound) they should put in their allowance together ; but she already felt the prospect quite weary and worn with the way he went round and round on it. It had become his sole topic, the theme alike of his most solemn prudences and most placid jests, to which every opening led for return and revision and in which every little flower of a foretaste was pulled up as soon as planted. He had announced at the earliest day — characterising the whole business, from that moment, as their " plans," under which name he handled it as a Syndicate handles a Chinese or other Loan — he had promptly declared that the question must be thoroughly studied, and he produced, on the whole subject,

F

from day to day, an amount of information that excited her wonder and even, not a little, as she frankly let him know, her disdain. When she thought of the danger in which another pair of lovers rapturously lived she enquired of him anew why he could leave nothing to chance. Then she got for answer that this profundity was just his pride, and he pitted Ramsgate against Bournemouth and even Boulogne against Jersey — for he had great ideas — with all the mastery of detail that was some day, professionally, to carry him afar.

The longer the time since she had seen Captain Everard the more she was booked, as she called it, to pass Park Chambers ; and this was the sole amusement that in the lingering August days and the twilights sadly drawn out it was left her to cultivate. She had long since learned to know it for a feeble one, though its feebleness was perhaps scarce the reason for her saying to herself each evening as her time for departure approached : " No, no — not to-night." She never failed of that silent remark, any more than she failed of feeling, in some deeper place than she had even yet fully sounded, that one's remarks were as weak as straws and that, however one might indulge in them at eight o'clock, one's fate infallibly declared itself in absolute indifference to them at about eight-fifteen. Remarks

were remarks, and very well for that; but fate
was fate, and this young lady's was to pass Park
Chambers every night in the working week. Out
of the immensity of her knowledge of the life of
the world there bloomed on these occasions as
specific remembrance that it was regarded in that
region, in August and September, as rather
pleasant just to be caught for something or other
in passing through town. Somebody was always
passing and somebody might catch somebody
else It was in full cognisance of this subtle
law that she adhered to the most ridiculous
circuit she could have made to get home. One
warm dull featureless Friday, when an accident
had made her start from Cocker's a little later
than usual, she became aware that something of
which the infinite possibilities had for so long
peopled her dreams was at last prodigiously
upon her, though the perfection in which the
conditions happened to present it was almost
rich enough to be but the positive creation of
a dream. She saw, straight before her, like a
vista painted in a picture, the empty street and
the lamps that burned pale in the dusk not
yet established. It was into the convenience of
this quiet twilight that a gentleman on the door-
step of the Chambers gazed with a vagueness
that our young lady's little figure violently

trembled, in the approach, with the measure of its power to dissipate. Everything indeed grew in a flash terrific and distinct ; her old uncertainties fell away from her, and, since she was so familiar with fate, she felt as if the very nail that fixed it were driven in by the hard look with which, for a moment, Captain Everard awaited her.

The vestibule was open behind him and the porter as absent as on the day she had peeped in ; he had just come out — was in town, in a tweed suit and a pot hat, but between two journeys — duly bored over his evening and at a loss what to do with it. Then it was that she was glad she had never met him in that way before : she reaped with such ecstasy the benefit of his not being able to think she passed often. She jumped in two seconds to the determination that he should even suppose it to be the very first time and the very oddest chance : this was while she still wondered if he would identify or notice her. His original attention had not, she instinctively knew, been for the young woman at Cocker's ; it had only been for any young woman who might advance to the tune of her not troubling the quiet air, and in fact the poetic hour, with ugliness. Ah but then, and just as she had reached the door, came his second observation, a long light reach with which, visibly and quite amusedly, he recalled and placed her. They were on different sides, but the street, narrow and still, had only made more of a stage for the small momentary drama. It was not over, besides, it was far from over, even on his sending across the way, with the pleasantest laugh she had ever heard, a little lift of his hat and an " Oh good evening ! " It was still less over on their meeting, the next minute, though rather indirectly and awkwardly, in the middle of the road — a situation to which three or four steps of her own had unmistakeably contributed — and then passing not again to the side on which she had arrived, but back toward the portal of Park Chambers.

" I did n't know you at first. Are you taking a walk ? "

" Ah I don't take walks at night ! I'm going home after my work."

" Oh ! "

That was practically what they had meanwhile smiled out, and his exclamation to which for a minute he appeared to have nothing to add, left them face to face and in just such an attitude as, for his part, he might have worn had he been wondering if he could properly ask her to come in. During this interval in fact she really felt his question to be just " *How* properly ——? " It was simply a question of the degree of properness.

XV

SHE never knew afterwards quite what she had done to settle it, and at the time she only knew that they presently moved, with vagueness, yet with continuity, away from the picture of the lighted vestibule and the quiet stairs and well up the street together. This also must have been in the absence of a definite permission, of anything vulgarly articulate, for that matter, on the part of either ; and it was to be, later on, a thing of remembrance and reflexion for her that the limit of what just here for a longish minute passed between them was his taking in her thoroughly successful deprecation, though conveyed without pride or sound or touch, of the idea that she might be, out of the cage, the very shopgirl at large that she hugged the theory she was n't. Yes, it was strange, she afterwards thought, that so much could have come and gone and yet not disfigured the dear little intense crisis either with impertinence or with resentment, with any of the horrid notes of that kind of acquaintance. He had taken no liberty, as she would have

86

called it; and, through not having to betray
the sense of one, she herself had, still more
charmingly, taken none. On the spot, nevertheless, she could speculate as to what it meant
that, if his relation with Lady Bradeen continued
to be what her mind had built it up to, he should
feel free to proceed with marked independence.
This was one of the questions he was to leave
her to deal with — the question whether people
of his sort still asked girls up to their rooms
when they were so awfully in love with other
women. Could people of his sort do that without
what people of *her* sort would call being " false
to their love " ? She had already a vision of
how the true answer was that people of her sort
did n't, in such cases, matter — did n't count
as infidelity, counted only as something else :
she might have been curious, since it came to
that, to see exactly what.

Strolling together slowly in their summer twilight and their empty corner of Mayfair, they
found themselves emerge at last opposite to one
of the smaller gates of the Park ; upon which,
without any particular word about it — they were
talking so of other things — they crossed the
street and went in and sat down on a bench.
She had gathered by this time one magnificent
hope about him—the hope he would say nothing

vulgar. She knew thoroughly what she meant by that; she meant something quite apart from any matter of his being "false." Their bench was not far within; it was near the Park Lane paling and the patchy lamplight and the rumbling cabs and 'buses. A strange emotion had come to her, and she felt indeed excitement within excitement; above all a conscious joy in testing him with chances he did n't take. She had an intense desire he should know the type she really conformed to without her doing anything so low as tell him, and he had surely begun to know it from the moment he did n't seize the opportunities into which a common man would promptly have blundered. These were on the mere awkward surface, and *their* relation was beautiful behind and below them. She had questioned so little on the way what they might be doing that as soon as they were seated she took straight hold of it. Her hours, her confinement, the many conditions of service in the post-office, had — with a glance at his own postal resources and alternatives — formed, up to this stage, the subject of their talk. "Well, here we are, and it may be right enough; but this is n't the least, you know, where I was going."

"You were going home?"

"Yes, and I was already rather late. I was going to my supper."

" You have n't had it ? "

" No indeed ! "

" Then you have n't eaten —— ? "

He looked of a sudden so extravagantly con‹
cerned that she laughed out. " All day ? Yes,
we do feed once. But that was long ago. So I
must pesently say good-bye."

" Oh deary *me !* " he exclaimed with an intonation so droll and yet a touch so light and a distress
so marked — a confession of helplessness for
such a case, in short, so unrelieved — that she
at once felt sure she had made the great difference
plain. He looked at her with the kindest eyes
and still without saying what she had known
he would n't. She had known he would n't say
" Then sup with *me !* " but the proof of it made
her feel as if she had feasted.

" I 'm not a bit hungry," she went on.

" Ah you *must* be, awfully ! " he made answer,
but settling himself on the bench as if, after all,
that need n't interfere with his spending his
evening. " I 've always quite wanted the chance
to thank you for the trouble you so often take
for me."

" Yes, I know," she replied ; uttering the words
with a sense of the situation far deeper than any
pretence of not fitting his allusion. She immediately felt him surprised and even a little puzzled

89

at her frank assent ; but for herself the trouble she had taken could only, in these fleeting minutes — they would probably never come back — be all there like a little hoard of gold in her lap. Certainly he might look at it, handle it, take up the pieces. Yet if he understood anything he must understand all. " I consider you 've already immensely thanked me." The horror was back upon her of having seemed to hang about for some reward. " It 's awfully odd you should have been there just the one time —— ! "

" The one time you 've passed my place ? "

" Yes ; you can fancy I have n't many minutes to waste. There was a place to-night I had to stop at."

" I see, I see " — he knew already so much about her work. " It must be an awful grind — for a lady."

" It is, but I don't think I groan over it any more than my companions — and you 've seen *they 're* not ladies ! " She mildly jested, but with an intention. " One gets used to things, and there are employments I should have hated much more." She had the finest conception of the beauty of not at least boring him. To whine, to count up her wrongs, was what a barmaid or a shopgirl would do, and it was quite enough to sit there like one of these.

" If you had had another employment," he

remarked after a moment, " we might never have become acquainted."

" It 's highly probable — and certainly not in the same way." Then, still with her heap of gold in her lap and something of the pride of it in her manner of holding her head, she continued not to move — she only smiled at him. The evening had thickened now ; the scattered lamps were red ; the Park, all before them, was full of obscure and ambiguous life ; there were other couples on other benches whom it was impossible not to see, yet at whom it was impossible to look. " But I 've walked so much out of my way with you only just to show you that — that " — with this she paused ; it was not after all so easy to express — " that anything you may have thought is perfectly true."

" Oh I 've thought a tremendous lot ! " her companion laughed. " Do you mind my smoking ? "

" Why should I ?   You always smoke *there*."

" At your place ?   Oh yes, but here it 's different."

" No," she said as he lighted a cigarette, " that 's just what it is n't. It 's quite the same."

" Well, then, that 's because ' there ' it 's so wonderful ! "

"Then you're conscious of how wonderful it is?" she returned.

He jerked his handsome head in literal protest at a doubt. "Why that's exactly what I mean by my gratitude for all your trouble. It has been just as if you took a particular interest." She only looked at him by way of answer in such sudden headlong embarrassment, as she was quite aware, that while she remained silent he showed himself checked by her expression. "You *have* — have n't you? — taken a particular interest?"

"Oh a particular interest!" she quavered out, feeling the whole thing — her headlong embarrassment — get terribly the better of her, and wishing, with a sudden scare, all the more to keep her emotion down. She maintained her fixed smile a moment and turned her eyes over the peopled darkness, unconfused now, because there was something much more confusing. This, with a fatal great rush, was simply the fact that they were thus together. They were near, near, and all she had imagined of that had only become more true, more dreadful and overwhelming. She stared straight away in silence till she felt she looked an idiot; then, to say something, to say nothing, she attempted a sound which ended in a flood of tears.

XVI

HER tears helped her really to dissimulate, for she had instantly, in so public a situation, to recover herself. They had come and gone in half a minute, and she immediately explained them. "It's only because I'm tired. It's that — it's that!" Then she added a trifle incoherently: "I shall never see you again."

"Ah but why not?" The mere tone in which her companion asked this satisfied her once for all as to the amount of imagination for which she could count on him. It was naturally not large: it had exhausted itself in having arrived at what he had already touched upon — the sense of an intention in her poor zeal at Cocker's. But any deficiency of this kind was no fault in him: *he* was n't obliged to have an inferior cleverness — to have second-rate resources and virtues. It had been as if he almost really believed she had simply cried for fatigue, and he accordingly put in some kind confused plea — "You ought really to take something: won't you have something or other *somewhere*?" — to which she had made no

response but a headshake of a sharpness that
settled it. " Why shan't we all the more keep
meeting ? "

" I mean meeting this way — only this way.
At my place there — *that* I 've nothing to do with,
and I hope of course you 'll turn up, with your
correspondence, when it suits you. Whether I
stay or not, I mean ; for I shall probably not
stay."

" You 're going somewhere else ? " — he put it
with positive anxiety.

" Yes, ever so far away — to the other end of
London. There are all sorts of reasons I can't
tell you ; and it 's practically settled. It 's better
for me, much ; and I 've only kept on at Cocker's
for *you*."

" For me ? "

Making out in the dusk that he fairly blushed,
she now measured how far he had been from knowing too much. Too much, she called it at present ;
and that was easy, since it proved so abundantly
enough for her that he should simply be where
he was. " As we shall never talk this way but
to-night — never, never again ! — here it all is.
I 'll say it ; I don't care what you think ; it
does n't matter ; I only want to help you. Besides, you 're kind — you 're kind. I 've been
thinking then of leaving for ever so long. But

you 've come so often — at times — and you 've
had so much to do, and it has been so pleasant and
interesting, that I 've remained, I 've kept putting
off any change. More than once, when I had
nearly decided, you 've turned up again and I 've
thought ' Oh no ! ' That 's the simple fact ! "
She had by this time got her confusion down so
completely that she could laugh. " This is what
I meant when I said to you just now that I
' knew.' I 've known perfectly that you knew I
took trouble for you ; and that knowledge has
been for me, and I seemed to see it was for you,
as if there were something — I don't know what
to call it ! — between us. I mean something
unusual and good and awfully nice — something
not a bit horrid or vulgar."

She had by this time, she could see, produced
a great effect on him ; but she would have
spoken the truth to herself had she at the same
moment declared that she did n't in the least
care : all the more that the effect must be one of
extreme perplexity. What, in it all, was visibly
clear for him, none the less, was that he was
tremendously glad he had met her. She held
him, and he was astonished at the force of it ;
he was intent, immensely considerate. His elbow
was on the back of the seat, and his head, with
the pot-hat pushed quite back, in a boyish way,

so that she really saw almost for the first time his forehead and hair, rested on the hand into which he had crumpled his gloves. "Yes," he assented, "it's not a bit horrid or vulgar."

She just hung fire a moment, then she brought out the whole truth. "I'd do anything for you. I'd do anything for you." Never in her life had she known anything so high and fine as this, just letting him have it and bravely and magnificently leaving it. Did n't the place, the associations and circumstances, perfectly make it sound what it was n't? and was n't that exactly the beauty?

So she bravely and magnificently left it, and little by little she felt him take it up, take it down, as if they had been on a satin sofa in a boudoir. She had never seen a boudoir, but there had been lots of boudoirs in the telegrams. What she had said at all events sank into him, so that after a minute he simply made a movement that had the result of placing his hand on her own — presently indeed that of her feeling herself firmly enough grasped. There was no pressure she need return, there was none she need decline; she just sat admirably still, satisfied for the time with the surprise and bewilderment of the impression she made on him. His agitation was even greater on the whole than she had at first allowed for. " I say, you know, you must n't think of leaving ! " he at last broke out.

" Of leaving Cocker's, you mean ? "

" Yes, you must stay on there, whatever happens, and help a fellow."

She was silent a little, partly because it was so strange and exquisite to feel him watch her as if it really mattered to him and he were almost in suspense. " Then you *have* quite recognised what I 've tried to do ? " she asked.

" Why, was n't that exactly what I dashed over from my door just now to thank you for ? "

" Yes ; so you said."

" And don't you believe it ? "

She looked down a moment at his hand, which continued to cover her own ; whereupon he presently drew it back, rather restlessly folding his arms. Without answering his question she went on : " Have you ever spoken of me ? "

" Spoken of you ? "

" Of my being there — of my knowing, and that sort of thing."

" Oh never to a human creature ! " he eagerly declared.

She had a small drop at this, which was expressed in another pause, and she then returned to what he had just asked her. " Oh yes, I quite believe you like it — my always being there and

our taking things up so familiarly and successfully : if not exactly where we left them," she
laughed, " almost always at least at an interesting point ! " He was about to say something in
reply to this, but her friendly gaiety was quicker.
" You want a great many things in life, a great
many comforts and helps and luxuries — you want
everything as pleasant as possible. Therefore,
so far as it 's in the power of any particular
person to contribute to all that —— " She had
turned her face to him smiling, just thinking.

" Oh see here ! " But he was highly amused.
" Well, what then ? " he enquired as if to humour
her.

" Why the particular person must never fail.
We must manage it for you somehow."

He threw back his head, laughing out ; he
was really exhilarated. " Oh yes, somehow ! "

" Well, I think we each do — don't we ? — in
one little way and another and according to our
limited lights. I 'm pleased at any rate, for
myself, that you are ; for I assure you I 've done
my best."

" You do better than any one ! " He had
struck a match for another cigarette, and the flame
lighted an instant his responsive finished face,
magnifying into a pleasant grimace the kindness
with which he paid her this tribute. " You 're

awfully clever, you know; cleverer, cleverer, cleverer —— ! " He had appeared on the point of making some tremendous statement; then suddenly, puffing his cigarette and shifting almost with violence on his seat, he let it altogether fall.

XVII

In spite of this drop, if not just by reason of it, she felt as if Lady Bradeen, all but named out, had popped straight up; and she practically betrayed her consciousness by waiting a little before she rejoined : " Cleverer than who ? "

" Well, if I was n't afraid you 'd think I swagger, I should say — than anybody ! If you leave your place there, where shall you go ? " he more gravely asked.

" Oh too far for you ever to find me ! "

" I 'd find you anywhere."

The tone of this was so still more serious that she had but her one acknowledgement. " I 'd do anything for you — I 'd do anything for you," she repeated. She had already, she felt, said it all ; so what did anything more, anything less, matter ? That was the very reason indeed why she could, with a lighter note, ease him generously of any awkwardness produced by solemnity, either his own or hers. " Of course it must be nice for you to be able to think there are people all about who feel in such a way."

In immediate appreciation of this, however, he only smoked without looking at her. "But you don't want to give up your present work?" he at last threw out. "I mean you *will* stay in the post-office?"

"Oh yes; I think I've a genius for that."

"Rather! No one can touch you." With this he turned more to her again. "But you can get, with a move, greater advantages?"

"I can get in the suburbs cheaper lodgings. I live with my mother. We need some space. There's a particular place that has other inducements."

He just hesitated. "Where is it?"

"Oh quite out of *your* way. You'd never have time."

"But I tell you I'd go anywhere. Don't you believe it?"

"Yes, for once or twice. But you'd soon see it wouldn't do for you."

He smoked and considered; seemed to stretch himself a little and, with his legs out, surrender himself comfortably. "Well, well, well — I believe everything you say. I take it from you — anything you like — in the most extraordinary way." It struck her certainly — and almost without bitterness — that the way in which she was already, as if she had been an old friend, arranging for him and preparing the only magnificence she could muster, was quite the most extraordinary. " Don't, *don't* go ! " he presently went on. " I shall miss you too horribly ! "

" So that you just put it to me as a definite request ? " — oh how she tried to divest this of all sound of the hardness of bargaining ! That ought to have been easy enough, for what was she arranging to get ? Before he could answer she had continued : " To be perfectly fair I should tell you I recognise at Cocker's certain strong attractions. All you people come. I like all the horrors."

" The horrors ? "

" Those you all — you know the set I mean, *your* set — show me with as good a conscience as if I had no more feeling than a letter-box."

He looked quite excited at the way she put it. " Oh they don't know ! "

" Don't know I 'm not stupid ? No, how should they ? "

" Yes, how should they ? " said the Captain sympathetically. " But is n't ' horrors ' rather strong ? "

" What you *do* is rather strong ! " the girl promptly returned.

" What *I* do ? "

"Your extravagance, your selfishness, your immorality, your crimes," she pursued, without heeding his expression.

"I *say !* " — her companion showed the queerest stare.

"I like them, as I tell you — I revel in them. But we need n't go into that," she quietly went on ; "for all I get out of it is the harmless pleasure of knowing. I know, I know, I know ! " — she breathed it ever so gently.

"Yes ; that 's what has been between us," he answered much more simply.

She could enjoy his simplicity in silence, and for a moment she did so. "If I do stay because you want it — and I 'm rather capable of that — there are two or three things I think you ought to remember. One is, you know, that I 'm there sometimes for days and weeks together without your ever coming."

"Oh I 'll come every day ! " he honestly cried.

She was on the point, at this, of imitating with her hand his movement of shortly before ; but she checked herself, and there was no want of effect in her soothing substitute. "How can you ? How can you ? " He had, too manifestly, only to look at it there, in the vulgarly animated gloom, to see that he could n't ; and at this point, by the mere action of his silence,

103

everything they had so definitely not named, the whole presence round which they had been circling, became part of their reference, settled in solidly between them. It was as if then for a minute they sat and saw it all in each other's eyes, saw so much that there was no need of a pretext for sounding it at last. " Your danger, your danger —— ! " Her voice indeed trembled with it, and she could only for the moment again leave it so.

During this moment he leaned back on the bench, meeting her in silence and with a face that grew more strange. It grew so strange that after a further instant she got straight up. She stood there as if their talk were now over, and he just sat and watched her. It was as if now — owing to the third person they had brought in — they must be more careful ; so that the most he could finally say was : " That 's where it is ! "

" That 's where it is ! " the girl as guardedly replied. He sat still, and she added : " I won't give you up. Good-bye."

" Good-bye ? " — he appealed, but without moving.

" I don't quite see my way, but I won't give you up," she repeated. " There. Good-bye."

It brought him with a jerk to his feet, tossing

away his cigarette. His poor face was flushed. " See here — see here ! "

" No, I won't ; but I must leave you now," she went on as if not hearing him.

" See here — see here ! " He tried, from the bench, to take her hand again.

But that definitely settled it for her : this would, after all, be as bad as his asking her to supper. " You must n't come with me — no, no ! "

He sank back, quite blank, as if she had pushed him. " I may n't see you home ? "

" No, no ; let me go." He looked almost as if she had struck him, but she did n't care ; and the manner in which she spoke — it was literally as if she were angry — had the force of a command. " Stay where you are ! "

" See here — see here ! " he nevertheless pleaded.

" I won't give you up ! " she cried once more — this time quite with passion ; on which she got away from him as fast as she could and left him staring after her.

XVIII

MR. MUDGE had lately been so occupied with their famous " plans " that he had neglected for a while the question of her transfer ; but down at Bournemouth, which had found itself selected as the field of their recreation by a process consisting, it seemed, exclusively of innumerable pages of the neatest arithmetic in a very greasy but most orderly little pocket-book, the distracting possible melted away — the fleeting absolute ruled the scene. The plans, hour by hour, were simply superseded, and it was much of a rest to the girl, as she sat on the pier and overlooked the sea and the company, to see them evaporate in rosy fumes and to feel that from moment to moment there was less left to cipher about. The week proved blissfully fine, and her mother, at their lodgings — partly to her embarrassment and partly to her relief — struck up with the landlady an alliance that left the younger couple a great deal of freedom. This relative took her pleasure of a week at Bournemouth in a stuffy back-kitchen and endless talks ; to that degree even

that Mr. Mudge himself — habitually inclined
indeed to a scrutiny of all mysteries and to seeing,
as he sometimes admitted, too much in things
— made remarks on it as he sat on the cliff
with his betrothed, or on the decks of steamers
that conveyed them, close-packed items in terrific
totals of enjoyment, to the Isle of Wight and
the Dorset coast.

He had a lodging in another house, where he
had speedily learned the importance of keeping
his eyes open, and he made no secret of his sus-
pecting that sinister mutual connivances might
spring, under the roof of his companions, from
unnatural sociabilities. At the same time he
fully recognised that as a source of anxiety, not
to say of expense, his future mother-in law would
have weighted them more by accompanying their
steps than by giving her hostess, in the interest
of the tendency they considered that they never
mentioned, equivalent pledges as to the tea-caddy
and the jam-pot. These were the questions —
these indeed the familiar commodities — that he
had now to put into the scales ; and his betrothed
had in consequence, during her holiday, the odd
and yet pleasant and almost languid sense of an
anticlimax. She had become conscious of an
extraordinary collapse, a surrender to stillness
and to retrospect. She cared neither to walk nor

to sail ; it was enough for her to sit on benches and wonder at the sea and taste the air and not be at Cocker's and not see the counter-clerk. She still seemed to wait for something — something in the key of the immense discussions that had mapped out their little week of idleness on the scale of a world-atlas. Something came at last, but without perhaps appearing quite adequately to crown the monument.

Preparation and precaution were, however, the natural flowers of Mr. Mudge's mind, and in proportion as these things declined in one quarter they inevitably bloomed elsewhere. He could always, at the worst, have on Tuesday the project of their taking the Swanage boat on Thursday, and on Thursday that of their ordering minced kidneys on Saturday. He had moreover a constant gift of inexorable enquiry as to where and what they should have gone and have done if they had n't been exactly as they were. He had in short his resources, and his mistress had never been so conscious of them ; on the other hand they never interfered so little with her own. She liked to be as she was — if it could only have lasted. She could accept even without bitterness a rigour of economy so great that the little fee they paid for admission to the pier had to be balanced against other delights.

The people at Ladle's and at Thrupp's had *their* ways of amusing themselves, whereas she had to sit and hear Mr. Mudge talk of what he might do if he did n't take a bath, or of the bath he might take if he only had n't taken something else. He was always with her now, of course, always beside her ; she saw him more than " hourly," more than ever yet, more even than he had planned she should do at Chalk Farm. She preferred to sit at the far end, away from the band and the crowd ; as to which she had frequent differences with her friend, who reminded her often that they could have only in the thick of it the sense of the money they were getting back. That had little effect on her, for she got back her money by seeing many things, the things of the past year, fall together and connect themselves, undergo the happy relegation that transforms melancholy and misery, passion and effort, into experience and knowledge.

She liked having done with them, as she assured herself she had practically done, and the strange thing was that she neither missed the procession now nor wished to keep her place for it. It had become there, in the sun and the breeze and the sea-smell, a far-away story, a picture of another life. If Mr. Mudge himself liked processions, liked them at Bournemouth and on the pier quite as much as at Chalk Farm or anywhere, she learned after a little not to be worried by his perpetual counting of the figures that made them up. There were dreadful women in particular, usually fat and in men's caps and white shoes, whom he could never let alone — not that *she* cared ; it was not the great world, the world of Cocker's and Ladle's and Thrupp's, but it offered an endless field to his faculties of memory, philosophy, and frolic. She had never accepted him so much, never arranged so successfully for making him chatter while she carried on secret conversations. This separate commerce was with herself ; and if they both practised a great thrift she had quite mastered that of merely spending words enough to keep him imperturbably and continuously going.

He was charmed with the panorama, not knowing — or at any rate not at all showing that he knew — what far other images peopled her mind than the women in the navy caps and the shopboys in the blazers. His observations on these types, his general interpretation of the show, brought home to her the prospect of Chalk Farm. She wondered sometimes that he should have derived so little illumination, during his period, from the society at Cocker's. But one evening while their holiday cloudlessly waned he gave her such a proof of his quality as might have made her ashamed of her many suppressions. He brought out something that, in all his overflow, he had been able to keep back till other matters were disposed of. It was the announcement that he was at last ready to marry — that he saw his way. A rise at Chalk Farm had been offered him ; he was to be taken into the business, bringing with him a capital the estimation of which by other parties constituted the handsomest recognition yet made of the head on his shoulders. Therefore their waiting was over — it could be a question of a near date. They would settle this date before going back, and he meanwhile had his eye on a sweet little home. He would take her to see it on their first Sunday.

XIX

His having kept this great news for the last, having had such a card up his sleeve and not floated it out in the current of his chatter and the luxury of their leisure, was one of those incalculable strokes by which he could still affect her; the kind of thing that reminded her of the latent force that had ejected the drunken soldier — an example of the profundity of which his promotion was the proof. She listened a while in silence, on this occasion, to the wafted strains of the music; she took it in as she had not quite done before that her future was now constituted. Mr. Mudge was distinctly her fate; yet at this moment she turned her face quite away from him, showing him so long a mere quarter of her cheek that she at last again heard his voice. He couldn't see a pair of tears that were partly the reason of her delay to give him the assurance he required; but he expressed at a venture the hope that she had had her fill of Cocker's.

She was finally able to turn back. "Oh quite. There's nothing going on. No one comes but the Americans at Thrupp's, and *they* don't do much. They don't seem to have a secret in the world."

"Then the extraordinary reason you 've been giving me for holding on there has ceased to work ? "

She thought a moment. "Yes, that one. I 've seen the thing through — I 've got them all in my pocket."

"So you 're ready to come ? "

For a little again she made no answer. "No, not yet, all the same. I 've still got a reason — a different one."

He looked her all over as if it might have been something she kept in her mouth or her glove or under her jacket — something she was even sitting upon. "Well, I 'll have it, please."

"I went out the other night and sat in the Park with a gentleman," she said at last.

Nothing was ever seen like his confidence in her ; and she wondered a little now why it did n't irritate her. It only gave her ease and space, as she felt, for telling him the whole truth that no one knew. It had arrived at present at her really wanting to do that, and yet to do it not in the least for Mr. Mudge, but altogether and only for herself. This truth filled out for her there the whole experience she was about to relinquish, suffused and coloured it as a picture that she should keep and that, describe it as she might, no one but herself would ever really see. Moreover she had no desire whatever to make Mr. Mudge jealous ; there would be no amusement in it, for the amusement she had lately known had spoiled her for lower pleasures. There were even no materials for it. The odd thing was how she never doubted that, properly handled, his passion was poisonable ; what had happened was that he had cannily selected a partner with no poison to distil. She read then and there that she should never interest herself in anybody as to whom some other sentiment, some superior view, would n't be sure to interfere for him with jealousy. "And what did you get out of that ? " he asked with a concern that was not in the least for his honour.

"Nothing but a good chance to promise him I would n't forsake him. He 's one of my customers."

"Then it 's for him not to forsake *you*."

"Well, he won't. It 's all right. But I must just keep on as long as he may want me."

"Want you to sit with him in the Park ? "

"He may want me for that — but I shan't. I rather liked it, but once, under the circumstances, is enough. I can do better for him in another manner."

" And what manner, pray ? "

" Well, elsewhere."

" Elsewhere ? — I *say* ! "

This was an ejaculation used also by Captain Everard, but oh with what a different sound ! " You need n't ' say ' — there 's nothing to be said. And yet you ought perhaps to know."

" Certainly I ought. But *what* — up to now ? "

" Why exactly what I told him. That I 'd do anything for him."

" What do you mean by ' anything ' ? "

" Everything."

Mr. Mudge's immediate comment on this statement was to draw from his pocket a crumpled paper containing the remains of half a pound of " sundries." These sundries had figured conspicuously in his prospective sketch of their tour, but it was only at the end of three days that they had defined themselves unmistakeably as chocolate-creams. " Have another ? — *that* one," he said. She had another, but not the one he indicated, and then he continued : " What took place afterwards ? "

" Afterwards ? "

" What did you do when you had told him you 'd do everything ? "

"I simply came away."

"Out of the Park?"

"Yes, leaving him there. I did n't let him follow me."

"Then what did you let him do?"

"I did n't let him do anything."

Mr. Mudge considered an instant. "Then what did you go there for?" His tone was even slightly critical.

"I did n't quite know at the time. It was simply to be with him, I suppose — just once. He 's in danger, and I wanted him to know I know it. It makes meeting him — at Cocker's, since it 's that I want to stay on for — more interesting."

"It makes it mighty interesting for *me!*" Mr. Mudge freely declared. "Yet he did n't follow you?" he asked. "*I* would!"

"Yes, of course. That was the way you began, you know. You 're awfully inferior to him."

"Well, my dear, you 're not inferior to anybody. You 've got a cheek! What 's he in danger of?"

"Of being found out. He 's in love with a lady — and it is n't right — and I 've found him out."

"That 'll be a look-out for *me!*" Mr. Mudge joked. "You mean she has a husband?"

" Never mind what she has ! They 're in awful danger, but his is the worst, because he 's in danger from her too."

" Like me from you — the woman *I* love ? If he 's in the same funk as me —— "

" He 's in a worse one. He 's not only afraid of the lady — he 's afraid of other things."

Mr. Mudge selected another chocolate-cream. " Well, I 'm only afraid of one ! But how in the world can you help this party ? "

" I don't know — perhaps not at all. But so long as there 's a chance —— "

" You won't come away ? "

" No, you 've got to wait for me."

Mr. Mudge enjoyed what was in his mouth. " And what will he give you ? "

" Give me ? "

" If you do help him."

" Nothing. Nothing in all the wide world."

" Then what will he give *me ?* " Mr. Mudge enquired. " I mean for waiting."

The girl thought a moment ; then she got up to walk. " He never heard of you," she replied.

" You have n't mentioned me ? "

" We never mention anything. What I 've told you is just what I 've found out."

Mr. Mudge, who had remained on the bench, looked up at her ; she often preferred to be quiet when he proposed to walk, but now that he seemed to wish to sit she had a desire to move. " But you have n't told me what *he* has found out."

She considered her lover. " He 'd never find *you*, my dear ! "

Her lover, still on his seat, appealed to her in something of the attitude in which she had last left Captain Everard, but the impression was not the same. " Then where do I come in ? "

" You don't come in at all. That 's just the beauty of it ! " — and with this she turned to mingle with the multitude collected round the band. Mr. Mudge presently overtook her and drew her arm into his own with a quiet force that expressed the serenity of possession ; in consonance with which it was only when they parted for the night at her door that he referred again to what she had told him

" Have you seen him since ? "

" Since the night in the Park ? No, not once."

" Oh, what a cad ! " said Mr. Mudge.

XX

It was not till the end of October that she saw
Captain Everard again, and on that occasion —
the only one of all the series on which hindrance
had been so utter — no communication with him
proved possible. She had made out even from
the cage that it was a charming golden day : a
patch of hazy autumn sunlight lay across the
sanded floor and also, higher up, quickened into
brightness a row of ruddy bottled syrups. Work
was slack and the place in general empty ; the
town, as they said in the cage, had not waked
up, and the feeling of the day likened itself to
something than in happier conditions she would
have thought of romantically as Saint Martin's
summer. The counter-clerk had gone to his
dinner ; she herself was busy with arrears of
postal jobs, in the midst of which she became
aware that Captain Everard had apparently
been in the shop a minute and that Mr. Buckton
had already seized him.

He had as usual half a dozen telegrams ; and
when he saw that she saw him and their eyes met

he gave, on bowing to her, an exaggerated laugh
in which she read a new consciousness. It was a
confession of awkwardness ; it seemed to tell her
that of course he knew he ought better to have
kept his head, ought to have been clever enough
to wait, on some pretext, till he should have
found her free. Mr. Buckton was a long time
with him, and her atention was soon demanded
by other visitors ; so that nothing passed between
them but the fulness of their silence. The look
she took from him was his greeting, and the
other one a simple sign of the eyes sent her
before going out. The only token they ex-
changed therefore was his tacit assent to her
wish that since they could n't attempt a certain
frankness they should attempt nothing at all.
This was her intense preference ; she could be as
still and cold as any one when that was the sole
solution.

Yet more than any contact hitherto achieved
these counted instants struck her as marking a
step : they were built so — just in the mere flash
— on the recognition of his now definitely knowing what it was she would do for him. The
" anything, anything " she had uttered in the
Park went to and fro between them and under
the poked-out chins that interposed. It had all
at last even put on the air of their not needing

now clumsily to manœuvre to converse : their
former little postal make-believes, the intense
implications of questions and answers and change,
had become in the light of the personal fact, of
their having had their moment, a possibility
comparatively poor. It was as if they had met
for all time — it exerted on their being in presence
again an influence so prodigious. When she
watched herself, in the memory of that night,
walk away from him as if she were making an
end, she found something too pitiful in the
primness of such a gait. Had n't she precisely
established on the part of each a consciousness
that could end only with death ?

It must be admitted that in spite of this
brave margin an irritation, after he had gone,
remained with her ; a sense that presently became
one with a still sharper hatred of Mr. Buckton,
who, on her friend's withdrawal, had retired
with the telegrams to the sounder and left her
the other work. She knew indeed she should
have a chance to see them, when she would, on
file ; and she was divided, as the day went on,
between the two impressions of all that was
lost and all that was re-asserted. What beset
her above all, and as she had almost never known
it before, was the desire to bound straight out,
to overtake the autumn afternoon before it

passed away for ever and hurry off to the Park and perhaps be with him there again on a bench. It became for an hour a fantastic vision with her that he might just have gone to sit and wait for her. She could almost hear him, through the tick of the sounder, scatter with his stick, in his impatience, the fallen leaves of October. Why should such a vision seize her at this particular moment with such a shake ? There was a time — from four to five — when she could have cried with happiness and rage.

Business quickened, it seemed, toward five, as if the town did wake up ; she had therefore more to do, and she went through it with little sharp stampings and jerkings : she made the crisp postal-orders fairly snap while she breathed to herself " It 's the last day — the last day ! " The last day of what ? She could n't have told. All she knew now was that if she *were* out of the cage she would n't in the least have minded, this time, its not yet being dark. She would have gone straignt toward Park Chambers and have hung about there till no matter when. She would have waited, stayed, rung, asked, have gone in, sat on the stairs. What the day was the last of was probably, to her strained inner sense, the group of golden ones, of any occasion for seeing the hazy sunshine slant at that angle into the smelly shop, of any range of chances for his wishing still to repeat to her the two words she had in the Park scarcely let him bring out. " See here — see here ! " — the sound of these two words had been with her perpetually ; but it was in her ears to-day without mercy, with a loudness that grew and grew. What was it they then expressed ? what was it he had wanted her to see ? She seemed, whatever it was, perfectly to see it now — to see that if she should just chuck the whole thing, should have a great and beautiful courage, he would somehow make everything up to her. When the clock struck five she was on the very point of saying to Mr. Buckton that she was deadly ill and rapidly getting worse. This announcement was on her lips, and she had quite composed the pale hard face she would offer him : " I can't stop — I must go home. If I feel better, later on, I 'll come back. I 'm very sorry, but I *must* go." At that instant Captain Everard once more stood there, producing in her agitated spirit, by his real presence, the strangest, quickest revolution. He stopped her off without knowing it, and by the time he had been a minute in the shop she felt herself saved.

That was from the first minute how she thought of it. There were again other persons with whom

she was occupied, and again the situation could
only be expressed by their silence. It was expressed, of a truth, in a larger phrase than ever
yet, for her eyes now spoke to him with a kind
of supplication. " Be quiet, be quiet ! " they
pleaded ; and they saw his own reply : " I 'll do
whatever you say ; I won't even look at you —
see, see ! " They kept conveying thus, with the
friendliest liberality, that they would n't look,
quite positively would n't. What she was to see
was that he hovered at the other end of the
counter, Mr. Buckton's end, and surrendered himself again to that frustration. It quickly proved
so great indeed that what she was to see further
was how he turned away before he was attended
to, and hung off, waiting, smoking, looking about
the shop ; how he went over to Mr. Cocker's own
counter and appeared to price things, gave in
fact presently two or three orders and put down
money, stood there a long time with his back to
her, considerately abstaining from any glance
round to see if she were free. It at last came
to pass in this way that he had remained in the
shop longer than she had ever yet known him
to do, and that, nevertheless, when he did turn
about she could see him time himself — she was
freshly taken up — and cross straight to her
postal subordinate, whom some one else had re-

leased. He had in his hand all this while neither letters nor telegrams, and now that he was close to her — for she was close to the counter-clerk — it brought her heart into her mouth merely to see him look at her neighbour and open his lips. She was too nervous to bear it. He asked for a Post-Office Guide, and the young man whipped out a new one; whereupon he said he wished not to purchase, but only to consult one a moment; with which, the copy kept on loan being produced, he once more wandered off.

What was he doing to her? What did he want of her? Well, it was just the aggravation of his "See here!" She felt at this moment strangely and portentously afraid of him — had in her ears the hum of a sense that, should it come to that kind of tension, she must fly on the spot to Chalk Farm. Mixed with her dread and with her reflexion was the idea that, if he wanted her so much as he seemed to show, it might be after all simply to do for him the "anything" she had promised, the "everything" she had thought it so fine to bring out to Mr. Mudge. He might want her to help him, might have some particular appeal; though indeed his manner did n't denote that — denoted on the contrary an embarrassment, an indecision, something of a desire not so much to be helped as to be treated rather more nicely than she had treated him the other time. Yes, he considered quite probably that he had help rather to offer than to ask for. Still, none the less, when he again saw her free he continued to keep away from her ; when he came back with his thumbed Guide it was Mr. Buckton he caught — it was from Mr. Buckton he obtained half-a-crown's-worth of stamps.

After asking for the stamps he asked, quite as a second thought, for a postal-order for ten shillings. What did he want with so many stamps when he wrote so few letters ? How could he enclose a postal-order in a telegram ? She expected him, the next thing, to go into the corner and make up one of his telegrams — half a dozen of them — on purpose to prolong his presence. She had so completely stopped looking at him that she could only guess his movements — guess even where his eyes rested. Finally she saw him make a dash that might have been toward the nook where the forms were hung ; and at this she suddenly felt that she could n't keep it up. The counter-clerk had just taken a telegram from a slavey, and, to give herself something to cover her, she snatched it out of his hand. The gesture was so violent that he gave her in return an odd look, and she also perceived that Mr. Buckton noticed it. The latter personage, with a quick stare at her, appeared for an instant to wonder whether his snatching it in *his* turn might n't be the thing she would least like, and she anticipated this practical criticism by the frankest glare she had ever given him. It sufficed : this time it paralysed him ; and she sought with her trophy the refuge of the sounder.

XXI

It was repeated the next day ; it went on for
three days ; and at the end of that time she
knew what to think. When, at the beginning,
she had emerged from her temporary shelter
Captain Everard had quitted the shop ; and he
had not come again that evening, as it had struck
her he possibly might — might all the more
easily that there were numberless persons who
came, morning and afternoon, numberless times,
so that he would n't necessarily have attracted
attention. The second day it was different and
yet on the whole worse. His access to her had
become possible — she felt herself even reaping
the fruit of her yesterday's glare at Mr. Buckton ;
but transacting his business with him did n't
simplify — it could, in spite of the rigour of
circumstance, feed so her new conviction. The
rigour was tremendous, and his telegrams — not
now mere pretexts for getting at her — were
apparently genuine ; yet the conviction had
taken but a night to develop. It could be simply
enough expressed ; she had had the glimmer

of it the day before in her idea that he needed
no more help than she had already given ; that
it was help he himself was prepared to render.
He had come up to town but for three or four
days ; he had been absolutely obliged to be absent
after the other time ; yet he would, now that he
was face to face with her, stay on as much longer
as she liked. Little by little it was thus clarified,
though from the first flash of his re-appearance
she had read into it the real essence.

That was what the night before, at eight
o'clock, her hour to go, had made her hang back
and dawdle. She did last things or pretended
to do them ; to be in the cage had suddenly
become her safety, and she was literally afraid
of the alternate self who might be waiting outside. *He* might be waiting ; it was he who was
her alternate self, and of him she was afraid.
The most extraordinary change had taken place
in her from the moment of her catching the
impression he seemed to have returned on purpose to give her. Just before she had done so,
on that bewitched afternoon, she had seen herself approach without a scruple the porter at
Park Chambers ; then as the effect of the rush
of a consciousness quite altered she had on at
last quitting Cocker's, gone straight home for
the first time since her return from Bourne-

mouth. She had passed his door every night
for weeks, but nothing would have induced her
to pass it now. This change was the tribute of
her fear — the result of a change in himself as to
which she needed no more explanation than his
mere face vividly gave her; strange though it
was to find an element of deterrence in the object
that she regarded as the most beautiful in the
world. He had taken it from her in the Park
that night that she wanted him not to propose
to her to sup; but he had put away the lesson
by this time — he practically proposed supper
every time he looked at her. This was what,
for that matter, mainly filled the three days.
He came in twice on each of these, and it was
as if he came in to give her a chance to relent.
That was after all, she said to herself in the
intervals, the most that he did. There were
ways, she fully recognised, in which he spared
her, and other particular ways as to which she
meant that her silence should be full to him of
exquisite pleading. The most particular of all
was his not being outside, at the corner, when she
quitted the place for the night. This he might
so easily have been — so easily if he had n't been
so nice. She continued to recognise in his forbearance the fruit of her dumb supplication, and
the only compensation he found for it was the

harmless freedom of being able to appear to say :
" Yes, I 'm in town only for three or four days,
but, you know, I *would* stay on." He struck her
as calling attention each day, each hour, to the
rapid ebb of time ; he exaggerated to the point of
putting it that there were only two days more,
that there was at last, dreadfully, only one.

There were other things still that he struck
her as doing with a special intention ; as to the
most marked of which — unless indeed it were
the most obscure — she might well have marvelled
that it did n't seem to her more horrid. It was
either the frenzy of her imagination or the dis-
order of his baffled passion that gave her once
or twice the vision of his putting down redundant
money — sovereigns not concerned with the little
payments he was perpetually making — so that
she might give him some sign of helping him to
slip them over to her. What was most extraordinary in this impression was the amount of
excuse that, with some incoherence, she found
for him. He wanted to pay her because there
was nothing to pay her for. He wanted to offer
her things he knew she would n't take. He
wanted to show her how much he respected her
by giving her the supreme chance to show *him*
she was respectable. Over the dryest transac-
tions, at any rate, their eyes had out these ques

tions. On the third day he put in a telegram
that had evidently something of the same point
as the stray sovereigns — a message that was in
the first place concocted and that on a second
thought he took back from her before she had
stamped it. He had given her time to read it
and had only then bethought himself that he
had better not send it. If it was not to Lady
Bradeen at Twindle — where she knew her ladyship then to be — this was because an address to
Doctor Buzzard at Brickwood was just as good,
with the added merit of its not giving away
quite so much a person whom he had still, after
all, in a manner to consider. It was of course
most complicated, only half lighted ; but there
was, discernibly enough, a scheme of communication in which Lady Bradeen at Twindle and
Dr. Buzzard at Brickwood were, within limits,
one and the same person. The words he had
shown her and then taken back consisted, at
all events, of the brief but vivid phrase " Absolutely impossible." The point was not that
she should transmit it ; the point was just
that she should see it. What was absolutely
impossible was that before he had setted something at Cocker's he should go either to Twindle
or to Brickwood.

The logic of this, in turn, for herself, was that

she could lend herself to no settlement so long
as she so intensely knew. What she knew was
that he was, almost under peril of life, clenched
in a situation : therefore how could she also
know where a poor girl in the P.O. might really
stand ? It was more and more between them
that if he might convey to her he was free, with all
the impossible locked away into a closed chapter,
her own case might become different for her, she
might understand and meet him and listen. But
he could convey nothing of the sort, and he only
fidgeted and floundered in his want of power.
The chapter was n't in the least closed, not for the
other party ; and the other party had a pull, somehow and somewhere : this his whole attitude and
expression confessed, at the same time that they
entreated her not to remember and not to mind.
So long as she did remember and did mind he
could only circle about and go and come, doing
futile things of which he was ashamed. He was
ashamed of his two words to Dr. Buzzard ;
he went out of the shop as soon as he had
crumpled up the paper again and thrust it into
his pocket. It had been an abject little exposure
of dreadful impossible passion. He appeared
in fact to be too ashamed to come back. He
had once more left town, and a first week elapsed,
and a second. He had had naturally to return

133

to the real mistress of his fate ; she had insisted
— she knew how to insist, and he could n't put in
another hour. There was always a day when she
called time. It was known to our young friend
moreover that he had now been dispatching telegrams from other offices. She knew at last so
much that she had quite lost her earlier sense of
merely guessing. There were no different shades
of distinctness — it all bounced out.

XXII

EIGHTEEN days elapsed, and she had begun to think it probable she should never see him again. He too then understood now : he had made out that she had secrets and reasons and impediments, that even a poor girl at the P.O. might have her complications. With the charm she had cast on him lightened by distance he had suffered a final delicacy to speak to him, had made up his mind that it would be only decent to let her alone. Never so much as during these latter days had she felt the precariousness of their relation — the happy beautiful untroubled original one, if it could only have been restored — in which the public servant and the casual public only were concerned. It hung at the best by the merest silken thread, which was at the mercy of any accident and might snap at any minute. She arrived by the end of the fortnight at the highest sense of actual fitness, never doubting that her decision was now complete. She would just give him a few days more to come back to her on a proper impersonal

basis — for even to an embarrassing representative
of the casual public a public servant with a
conscience did owe something — and then would
signify to Mr. Mudge that she was ready for the
little home. It had been visited, in the further
talk she had had with him at Bournemouth,
from garret to cellar, and they had especially
lingered, with their respectively darkened brows,
before the niche into which it was to be broached
to her mother that she must find means to fit.

He had put it to her more definitely than
before that his calculations had allowed for that
dingy presence, and he had thereby marked the
greatest impression he had ever made on her.
It was a stroke superior even again to his handling
of the drunken soldier. What she considered
that in the face of it she hung on at Cocker's
for was something she could only have described
as the common fairness of a last word. Her actual
last word had been, till it should be superseded,
that she would n't forsake her other friend, and it
stuck to her through thick and thin that she was
still at her post and on her honour. This other
friend had shown so much beauty of conduct
already that he would surely after all just re-appear
long enough to relieve her, to give her something
she could take away. She saw it, caught it, at
times, his parting present ; and there were

moments when she felt herself sitting like a beggar with a hand held out to an almsgiver who only fumbled. She had n't taken the sovereigns, but she *would* take the penny. She heard, in imagination, on the counter, the ring of the copper. "Don't put yourself out any longer," he would say, "for so bad a case. You 've done all there is to be done. I thank and acquit and release you. Our lives take us. I don't know much — though I 've really been interested — about yours, but I suppose you 've got one. Mine at any rate will take *me* — and where it will. Heigh-ho! Good-bye." And then once more, for the sweetest faintest flower of all: "Only, I say — see here!" She had framed the whole picture with a squareness that included also the image of how again she would decline to "see there," decline, as she might say, to see anywhere, see anything. Yet it befell that just in the fury of this escape she saw more than ever.

He came back one night with a rush, near the moment of their closing, and showed her a face so different and new, so upset and anxious, that almost anything seemed to look out of it but clear recognition. He poked in a telegram very much as if the simple sense of pressure, the distress of extreme haste, had blurred the remembrance of where in particular he was. But as she met his eyes a light came ; it broke indeed on the spot into a positive conscious glare. That made up for everything, since it was an instant proclamation of the celebrated " danger " ; it seemed to pour things out in a flood. " Oh yes, here it is — it 's upon me at last ! Forget, for God's sake, my having worried or bored you, and just help me, just *save* me, by getting this off without the loss of a second ! " Something grave had clearly occurred, a crisis declared itself. She recognised immediately the person to whom the telegram was addressed — the Miss Dolman of Parade Lodge to whom Lady Bradeen had wired, at Dover, on the last occasion, and whom she had then, with her recollection of previous arrangements, fitted into a particular setting. Miss Dolman had figured before and not figured since, but she was now the subject of an imperative appeal. " Absolutely necessary to see you. Take last train Victoria if you can catch it. If not, earliest morning, and answer me direct either way."

" Reply paid ? " said the girl. Mr. Buckton had just departed and the counter-clerk was at the sounder. There was no other representative of the public, and she had never yet, as it seemed to her, not even in the street or in the Park, been so alone with him.

"Oh yes, reply paid, and as sharp as possible, please."

She affixed the stamps in a flash. "She 'll catch the train!" she then declared to him breathlessly, as if she could absolutely guarantee it.

"I don't know — I hope so. It 's awfully important. So kind of you. Awfully sharp, please." It was wonderfully innocent now, his oblivion of all but his danger. Anything else that had ever passed between them was utterly out of it. Well, she had wanted him to be impersonal!

There was less of the same need therefore, happily, for herself; yet she only took time, before she flew to the sounder, to gasp at him: "You 're in trouble?"

"Horrid, horrid — there 's a row!" But they parted, on it, in the next breath; and as she dashed at the sounder, almost pushing, in her violence, the counter-clerk off the stool, she caught the bang with which, at Cocker's door, in his further precipitation, he closed the apron of the cab into which he had leaped. As he rebounded to some other precaution suggested by his alarm, his appeal to Miss Dolman flashed straight away.

But she had not, on the morrow, been in the

place five minutes before he was with her again, still more discomposed and quite, now, as she said to herself, like a frightened child coming to its mother. Her companions were there, and she felt it to be remarkable how, in the presence of his agitation, his mere scared exposed nature, she suddenly ceased to mind. It came to her as it had never come to her before that with absolute directness and assurance they might carry almost anything off. He had nothing to send — she was sure he had been wiring all over — and yet his business was evidently huge. There was nothing but that in his eyes — not a glimmer of reference or memory. He was almost haggard with anxiety and had clearly not slept a wink. Her pity for him would have given her any courage, and she seemed to know at last why she had been such a fool. " She didn't come ? " she panted.

" Oh yes, she came ; but there has been some mistake. We want a telegram."

" A telegram ? "

" One that was sent from here ever so long ago. There was something in it that has to be recovered. Something very, *very* important, please — we want it immediately."

He really spoke to her as if she had been some strange young woman at Knightsbridge or Pad-

dington ; but it had no other effect on her than
to give her the measure of his tremendous flurry.
Then it was that, above all, she felt how much
she had missed in the gaps and blanks and absent
answers — how much she had had to dispense
with : it was now black darkness save for this
little wild red flare. So much as that she saw,
so much her mind dealt with. One of the lovers
was quaking somewhere out of town, and the
other was quaking just where he stood. This was
vivid enough, and after an instant she knew it was
all she wanted. She wanted no detail, no fact —
she wanted no nearer vision of discovery or shame.
" When was your telegram ? Do you mean you
sent it from here ? " She tried to do the young
woman at Knightsbridge.

" Oh yes, from here — several weeks ago. Five,
six, seven " — he was confused and impatient —
" don't you remember ? "

" Remember ? " she could scarcely keep out of
her face, at the word, the strangest of smiles.

But the way he did n't catch what it meant
was perhaps even stranger still. " I mean, don't
you keep the old ones ? "

" For a certain time."

" But how long ? "

She thought ; she *must* do the young woman,
and she knew exactly what the young woman

would say and, still more, would n't. " Can you
give me the date ? "

" Oh God, no ! It was some time or other in
August — toward the end. It was to the same
address as the one I gave you last night."

" Oh ! " said the girl, knowing at this the deepest thrill she had ever felt. It came to her there,
with her eyes on his face, that she held the whole
thing in her hand, held it as she held her pencil,
which might have broken at that instant in her
tightened grip. This made her feel like the very
fountain of fate, but the emotion was such a
flood that she had to press it back with all her
force. That was positively the reason, again, of
her flute-like Paddington tone. " You can't give
us anything a little nearer ? " Her " little " and
her " us " came straight from Paddington. These
things were no false note for him — his difficulty
absorbed them all. The eyes with which he
pressed her, and in the depths of which she read
terror and rage and literal tears, were just the
same he would have shown any other prim person.

" I don't know the date. I only know the thing
went from here, and just about the time I speak
of. It was n't delivered, you see. We 've got to
recover it "

XXIII

She was as struck with the beauty of his plural pronoun as she had judged he might be with that of her own ; but she knew now so well what she was about that she could almost play with him and with her new-born joy. " You say ' about the time you speak of.' But I don't think you speak of an exact time — *do* you ? "

He looked splendidly helpless. " That 's just what I want to find out. Don't you keep the old ones ? — can't you look it up ? "

Our young lady — still at Paddington — turned the question over. " It was n't delivered ? "

" Yes, it *was ;* yet, at the same time, don't you know ? it was n't." He just hung back, but he brought it out. " I mean it was intercepted, don't you know ? and there was something in it." He paused again and, as if to further his quest and woo and supplicate success and recovery, even smiled with an effort at the agreeable that was almost ghastly and that turned the knife in her tenderness. What must be the pain of it all, of the open gulf and the throbbing fever, when this

143

was the mere hot breath? "We want to get what was in it — to know what it was."

"I see — I see." She managed just the accent they had at Paddington when they stared like dead fish. "And you have no clue?"

"Not at all — I 've the clue I 've just given you."

"Oh the last of August?" If she kept it up long enough she would make him really angry.

"Yes, and the address, as I 've said."

"Oh the same as last night?"

He visibly quivered, as with a gleam of hope; but it only poured oil on her quietude, and she was still deliberate. She ranged some papers. "Won't you look?" he went on.

"I remember your coming," she replied.

He blinked with a new uneasiness; it might have begun to come to him, through her difference, that he was somehow different himself. "You were much quicker then, you know!"

"So were you — you must do me that justice," she answered with a smile. "But let me see. Was n't it Dover?"

"Yes, Miss Dolman ——"

"Parade Lodge, Parade Terrace?"

"Exactly — thank you so awfully much!" He began to hope again. "Then you *have* it — the other one?"

144

She hesitated afresh ; she quite dangled him.
" It was brought by a lady ? "

" Yes ; and she put in by mistake something
wrong. That 's what we 've got to get hold of ! "
Heavens, what was he going to say ? — flood-
ing poor Paddington with wild betrayals ! She
could n't too much, for her joy, dangle him, yet
she could n't either, for his dignity, warn or con-
trol or check him. What she found herself doing
was just to treat herself to the middle way. " It
was intercepted ? "

" It fell into the wrong hands. But there 's
something in it," he continued to blurt out,
" that *may* be all right. That is, if it 's wrong,
don't you know ? It 's all right if it 's wrong,"
he remarkably explained.

What *was* he, on earth, going to say ? Mr.
Buckton and the counter-clerk were already
interested ; no one *would* have the decency to
come in ; and she was divided between her particular terror for him and her general curiosity.
Yet she already saw with what brilliancy she could
add, to carry the thing off, a little false knowledge
to all her real. " I quite understand," she said
with benevolent, with almost patronising quick-
ness. " The lady has forgotten what she did put."

" Forgotten most wretchedly, and it 's an immense inconvenience. It has only just been

K

found that it did n't get there ; so that if we could immediately have it —— "

" Immediately ? "

" Every minute counts. You *have*," he pleaded, " surely got them on file ? "

" So that you can see it on the spot ? "

" Yes, please — this very minute." The counter rang with his knuckles, with the knob of his stick, with his panic of alarm. " Do, *do* hunt it up ! " he repeated.

"I dare say we could get it for you," the girl weetly returned.

" Get it ? " — he looked aghast. " When ? "

" Probably by to-morrow."

" Then it is n't here ? " — his face was pitiful.

She caught only the uncovered gleams that peeped out of the blackness, and she wondered what complication, even among the most supposable, the very worst, could be bad enough to account for the degree of his terror. There were twists and turns, there were places where the screw drew blood, that she could n't guess. She was more and more glad she did n't want to. " It has been sent on."

" But how do you know if you don't look ? "

She gave him a smile that was meant to be, in the absolute irony of its propriety, quite

146

divine. " It was August 23rd, and we 've nothing
later here than August 27th."

Something leaped into his face. " 27th —
23rd ? Then you 're sure ? You know ? "

She felt she scarce knew what — as if she might
soon be pounced upon for some lurid connexion
with a scandal. It was the queerest of all sensa-
tions, for she had heard, she had read, of these
things, and the wealth of her intimacy with
them at Cocker's might be supposed to have
schooled and seasoned her. This particular one
that she had really quite lived with was, after
all, an old story ; yet what it had been before
was dim and distant beside the touch under
which she now winced. Scandal ? — it had never
been but a silly word. Now it was a great tense
surface, and the surface was somehow Captain
Everard's wonderful face. Deep down in his
eyes a picture, a scene — a great place like a
chamber of justice, where, before a watching
crowd, a poor girl, exposed but heroic, swore with
a quavering voice to a document, proved an *alibi*,
supplied a link. In this picture she bravely took
her place. " It was the 23rd."

" Then can't you get it this morning — or some
time to-day ? "

She considered, still holding him with her look,
which she then turned on her two companions,

who were by this time unreservedly enlisted.
She did n't care — not a scrap, and she glanced
about for a piece of paper. With this she had to
recognise the rigour of official thrift — a morsel
of blackened blotter was the only loose paper to
be seen. " Have you got a card ? " she said to
her visitor. He was quite away from Paddington
now, and the next instant, pocket-book in hand,
he had whipped a card out. She gave no glance
at the name on it — only turned it to the other
side. She continued to hold him, she felt at
present, as she had never held him ; and her
command of her colleagues was for the moment
not less marked. She wrote something on the
back of the card and pushed it across to him.

He fairly glared at it. " Seven, nine,
four —— "

" Nine, six, one " — she obligingly completed
the number. " Is it right ? " she smiled.

He took the whole thing in with a flushed
intensity ; then there broke out in him a visi-
bility of relief that was simply a tremendous
exposure. He shone at them all like a tall
lighthouse, embracing even, for sympathy, the
blinking young men. " By all the powers — it 's
wrong ! " And without another look, without
a word of thanks, without time for anything
or anybody, he turned on them the broad back

of his great stature, straightened his triumphant shoulders, and strode out of the place.

She was left confronted with her habitual critics. "'If it's wrong it's all right!'" she extravagantly quoted to them.

The counter-clerk was really awe-stricken. "But how did you know, dear?"

"I remembered, love!"

Mr. Buckton, on the contrary, was rude. "And what game is that, miss?"

No happiness she had ever known came within miles of it, and some minutes elapsed before she could recall herself sufficiently to reply that it was none of his business.

XXIV

IF life at Cocker's, with the dreadful drop of August, had lost something of its savour, she had not been slow to infer that a heavier blight had fallen on the graceful industry of Mrs. Jordan. With Lord Rye and Lady Ventnor and Mrs. Bubb all out of town, with the blinds down on all the homes of luxury, this ingenious woman might well have found her wonderful taste left quite on her hands. She bore up, however, in a way that began by exciting much of her young friend's esteem ; they perhaps even more frequently met as the wine of life flowed less free from other sources, and each, in the lack of better diversion, carried on with more mystification for the other an intercourse that consisted not a little in peeping out and drawing back. Each waited for the other to commit herself, each profusely curtained for the other the limits of low horizons. Mrs. Jordan was indeed probably the more reckless skirmisher ; nothing could exceed her frequent incoherence unless it was indeed her occasional bursts of confidence. Her

account of her private affairs rose and fell like a
flame in the wind — sometimes the bravest bon-
fire and sometimes a handful of ashes. This our
young woman took to be an effect of the position,
at one moment and another, of the famous door
of the great world. She had been struck in one
of her ha'penny volumes with the translation of
a French proverb according to which such a
door, any door, had to be either open or shut ; and
it seemed part of the precariousness of Mrs.
Jordan's life that hers mostly managed to be
neither. There had been occasions when it appeared to gape wide — fairly to woo her across
its threshold ; there had been others, of an order
distinctly disconcerting, when it was all but
banged in her face. On the whole, however,
she had evidently not lost heart ; these still
belonged to the class of things in spite of which
she looked well. She intimated that the profits
of her trade had swollen so as to float her through
any state of the tide, and she had, besides this,
a hundred profundities and explanations.

She rose superior, above all, on the happy
fact that there were always gentlemen in town
and that gentlemen were her greatest admirers ;
gentlemen from the City in especial — as to
whom she was full of information about the
passion and pride excited in such breasts by the

elements of her charming commerce. The City
men *did* in short go in for flowers. There was
a certain type of awfully smart stockbroker —
Lord Rye called them Jews and bounders, but
she did n't care — whose extravagance, she more
than once threw out, had really, if one had any
conscience, to be forcibly restrained. It was not
perhaps a pure love of beauty : it was a matter
of vanity and a sign of business ; they wished to
crush their rivals, and that was one of their
weapons. Mrs. Jordan's shrewdness was extreme ;
she knew in any case her customer — she dealt, as
she said, with all sorts ; and it was at the worst
a race for her — a race even in the dull months
— from one set of chambers to another. And
then, after all, there were also still the ladies ; the
ladies of stockbroking circles were perpetually up
and down. They were not quite perhaps Mrs.
Bubb or Lady Ventnor ; but you could n't tell
the difference unless you quarrelled with them, and
then you knew it only by their making-up sooner.
These ladies formed the branch of her subject on
which she most swayed in the breeze ; to that
degree that her confidant had ended with an
inference or two tending to banish regret for
opportunities not embraced. There were indeed
tea-gowns that Mrs. Jordan described — but tea-
gowns were not the whole of respectability, and

it was odd that a clergyman's widow should sometimes speak as if she almost thought so. She came back, it was true, unfailingly to Lord Rye, never, evidently, quite losing sight of him even on the longest excursions. That he was kindness itself had become in fact the very moral it all pointed — pointed in strange flashes of the poor woman's nearsighted eyes. She launched at her young friend portentous looks, solemn heralds of some extraordinary communication. The communication itself, from week to week, hung fire ; but it was to the facts over which it hovered that she owed her power of going on. "They are, in one way *and* another," she often emphasised, " a tower of strength " ; and as the allusion was to the aristocracy the girl could quite wonder why, if they were so in " one way," they should require to be so in two. She thoroughly knew, however, how many ways Mrs. Jordan counted in. It all meant simply that her fate was pressing her close. If that fate was to be sealed at the matrimonial altar it was perhaps not remarkable that she should n't come all at once to the scratch of overwhelming a mere telegraphist. It would necessarily present to such a person a prospect of regretful sacrifice. Lord Rye — if it *was* Lord Rye — would n't be " kind " to a nonentity of that sort, even though people quite as good had been.

One Sunday afternoon in November they went, by arrangement, to church together ; after which — on the inspiration of the moment the arrangement had not included it — they proceeded to Mrs. Jordan's lodging in the region of Maida Vale. She had raved to her friend about her service of predilection ; she was excessively "high," and had more than once wished to introduce the girl to the same comfort and privilege. There was a thick brown fog and Maida Vale tasted of acrid smoke ; but they had been sitting among chants and incense and wonderful music, during which, though the effect of such things on her mind was great, our young lady had indulged in a series of reflexions but indirectly related to them. One of these was the result of Mrs. Jordan's having said to her on the way, and with a certain fine significance, that Lord Rye had been for some time in town. She had spoken as if it were a circumstance to which little required to be added — as if the bearing of such an item on her life might easily be grasped. Perhaps it was the wonder of whether Lord Rye wished to marry her that made her guest, with thoughts straying to that quarter, quite determine that some other nuptials also should take place at Saint Julian's. Mr. Mudge was still an attendant at his Wesleyan chapel, but this was the least of her worries — it had never even vexed her enough for her to so much as name it to Mrs. Jordan. Mr. Mudge's form of worship was one of several things — they made up in superiority and beauty for what they wanted in number — that she had long ago settled he should take from her, and she had now moreover for the first time definitely established her own. Its principal feature was that it was to be the same as that of Mrs. Jordan and Lord Rye ; which was indeed very much what she said to her hostess as they sat together later on. The brown fog was in this hostess's little parlour, where it acted as a postponement of the question of there being, besides, anything else than the teacups and a pewter pot and a very black little fire and a paraffin lamp without a shade. There was at any rate no sign of a flower ; it was not for herself Mrs. Jordan gathered sweets. The girl waited till they had had a cup of tea — waited for the announcement that she fairly believed her friend had, this time, possessed herself of her formally at last to make ; but nothing came, after the interval, save a little poke at the fire, which was like the clearing of a throat for a speech.

XXV

" I THINK you must have heard me speak of
Mr. Drake ? " Mrs. Jordan had never looked so
queer, nor her smile so suggestive of a large
benevolent bite.

"Mr. Drake ? Oh yes ; is n't he a friend of
Lord Rye ? "

" A great and trusted friend. Almost — I may
say — a loved friend."

Mrs. Jordan's " almost " had such an oddity
that her companion was moved, rather flippantly
perhaps, to take it up. " Don't people as
good as love their friends when they ' trust '
them ? "

It pulled up a little the eulogist of Mr. Drake.
" Well, my dear, I love *you* ——"

" But you don't trust me ? " the girl unmerci-
fully asked.

Again Mrs. Jordan paused — still she looked
queer. " Yes," she replied with a certain austerity ; " that 's exactly what I 'm about to give
you rather a remarkable proof of." The sense
of its being remarkable was already so strong

that, while she bridled a little, this held her auditor in a momentary muteness of submission. " Mr. Drake has rendered his lordship for several years services that his lordship has highly appreciated and that make it all the more — a — unexpected that they should, perhaps a little suddenly, separate."

" Separate ? " Our young lady was mystified, but she tried to be interested ; and she already saw that she had put the saddle on the wrong horse. She had heard something of Mr. Drake, who was a member of his lordship's circle — the member with whom, apparently, Mrs. Jordan's avocations had most happened to throw her. She was only a little puzzled at the " separation." " Well, at any rate," she smiled, " if they separate as friends —— ! "

" Oh his lordship takes the greatest interest in Mr. Drake's future. He 'll do anything for him ; he has in fact just done a great deal. There *must*, you know, be changes —— ! "

" No one knows it better than I," the girl said. She wished to draw her interlocutress out. " There will be changes enough for me."

" You 're leaving Cocker's ? "

The ornament of that establishment waited a moment to answer, and then it was indirect. " Tell me what *you 're* doing."

157

"Well, what will you think of it ? "

"Why that you 've found the opening you were always so sure of."

Mrs. Jordan, on this, appeared to muse with embarrassed intensity. " I was always sure, yes — and yet I often was n't ! "

"Well, I hope you 're sure now. Sure, I mean, of Mr. Drake."

"Yes, my dear, I think I may say I *am*. I kept him going till I was."

"Then he 's yours ? "

"My very own."

"How nice ! And awfully rich ? " our young woman went on.

Mrs. Jordan showed promptly enough that she loved for higher things. "Awfully handsome — six foot two. And he *has* put by."

"Quite like Mr. Mudge, then ! " that gentleman's friend rather desperately exclaimed.

"Oh not *quite !* " Mr. Drake's was ambiguous about it, but the name of Mr. Mudge had evidently given her some sort of stimulus. "He 'll have more opportunity now, at any rate. He 's going to Lady Bradeen."

"To Lady Bradeen ? " This was bewilderment. "' Going —— ' ? "

The girl had seen, from the way Mrs. Jordan looked at her, that the effect of the name had been to make her let something out. " Do you know her ? "

She floundered, but she found her feet. " Well, you 'll remember I 've often told you that if you 've grand clients I have them too."

" Yes," said Mrs. Jordan ; " but the great difference is that you hate yours, whereas I really love mine. *Do* you know Lady Bradeen ? " she pursued.

" Down to the ground ! She 's always in and out."

Mrs. Jordan's foolish eyes confessed, in fixing themselves on this sketch, to a degree of wonder and even of envy. But she bore up and, with a certain gaiety, " Do you hate *her ?* " she demanded.

Her visitor's reply was prompt. " Dear no ! — not nearly so much as some of them. She 's too outrageously beautiful."

Mrs. Jordan continued to gaze. " Outrageously ? "

" Well, yes ; deliciously." What was really delicious was Mrs. Jordan's vagueness. " You don't know her — you 've not seen her ? " her guest lightly continued.

" No, but I 've heard a great deal about her."

" So have I ! " our young lady exclaimed.

Mrs. Jordan looked an instant as if she suspected her good faith, or at least her seriousness. " You know some friend —— ? "

" Of Lady Bradeen's ? Oh yes — I know one."

" Only one ? "

The girl laughed out. " Only one — but he 's so intimate."

Mrs. Jordan just hesitated. " He 's a gentleman ? "

" Yes, he 's not a lady."

Her interlocutress appeared to muse. " She 's immensely surrounded."

" She *will* be — with Mr. Drake ! "

Mrs. Jordan's gaze became strangely fixed. " Is she *very* good-looking ? "

" The handsomest person I know."

Mrs. Jordan continued to brood. " Well, *I* know some beauties." Then with her odd jerkiness : " Do you think she looks *good* ? "

" Because that 's not always the case with the good-looking ? " — the other took it up. " No, indeed, it is n't : that 's one thing Cocker's has taught me. Still, there are some people who have everything. Lady Bradeen, at any rate, has enough : eyes and a nose and a mouth, a complexion, a figure —— "

" A figure ? " Mrs. Jordan almost broke in.

" A figure, a head of hair ! " The girl made a little conscious motion that seemed to let the hair all down, and her companion watched the wonderful show. " But Mr. Drake *is* another —— ? "

" Another ? " — Mrs. Jordan's thoughts had to come back from a distance.

" Of her ladyship's admirers. He 's ' going,' you say, to her ? "

At this Mrs. Jordan really faltered. " She has engaged him."

" Engaged him ? " — our young woman was quite at sea.

" In the same capacity as Lord Rye."

" And was Lord Rye engaged ? "

XXVI

Mrs. Jordan looked away from her now — looked, she thought, rather injured and, as if trifled with, even a little angry. The mention of Lady Bradeen had frustrated for a while the convergence of our heroine's thoughts ; but with this impression of her old friend's combined impatience and diffidence they began again to whirl round her, and continued it till one of them appeared to dart at her, out of the dance, as if with a sharp peck. It came to her with a lively shock, with a positive sting, that Mr. Drake was — could it be possible ? With the idea she found herself afresh on the edge of laughter, of a sudden and strange perversity of mirth. Mr. Drake loomed, in a swift image, before her ; such a figure as she had seen in open doorways of houses in Cocker's quarter — majestic, middle-aged, erect, flanked on either side by a footman and taking the name of a visitor. Mr. Drake then verily *was* a person who opened the door ! Before she had time, however, to recover from the effect of her evocation, she was offered a vision which

quite engulfed it. It was communicated to
her somehow that the face with which she had
seen it rise prompted Mrs. Jordan to dash, a bit
wildly, at something, at anything, that might at-
tenuate criticism. " Lady Bradeen 's re-arranging
— she 's going to be married."

" Married ? " The girl echoed it ever so softly,
but there it was at last.

" Did n't you know it ? "

She summoned all her sturdiness. " No, she
has n't told me."

" And her friends — have n't they ? "

" I have n't seen any of them lately. I 'm not
so fortunate as *you*."

Mrs. Jordan gathered herself. " Then you
have n't even heard of Lord Bradeen's death ? "

Her comrade, unable for a moment to speak,
gave a slow headshake. " You know it from
Mr. Drake ? " It was better surely not to learn
things at all than to learn them by the butler.

" She tells him everything."

" And he tells *you* — I see." Our young lady
got up ; recovering her muff and her gloves she
smiled. " Well, I have n't unfortunately any
Mr. Drake. I congratulate you with all my
heart. Even without your sort of assistance,
however, there 's a trifle here and there that
I do pick up. I gather that if she 's to

marry any one it must quite necessarily be my friend."

Mrs. Jordan was now also on her feet. " Is Captain Everard your friend ? "

The girl considered, drawing on a glove " I saw, at one time, an immense deal of him."

Mrs. Jordan looked hard at the glove, but she had n't after all waited for that to be sorry it was n't cleaner. " What time was that ? "

" It must have been the time you were seeing so much of Mr. Drake." She had now fairly taken it in : the distinguished person Mrs. Jordan was to marry would answer bells and put on coals and superintend, at least, the cleaning of boots for the other distinguished person whom *she* might — well, whom she might have had, if she had wished, so much more to say to. " Good-bye," she added ; " good-bye."

Mrs. Jordan, however, again taking her muff from her, turned it over, brushed it off and thoughtfully peeped into it. " Tell me this before you go. You spoke just now of your own changes. Do you mean that Mr. Mudge —— ? "

" Mr. Mudge has had great patience with me — he has brought me at last to the point. We 're to be married next month and have a nice little home. But he 's only a grocer, you know " — the girl met her friend's intent eyes — " so that I 'm afraid that, with the set you 've got into, you won't see your way to keep up our friendship."

Mrs. Jordan for a moment made no answer to this ; she only held the muff up to her face, after which she gave it back. "You don't like it. I see, I see."

To her guest's astonishment there were tears now in her eyes. "I don't like what ?" the girl asked.

"Why my engagement. Only, with your great cleverness," the poor lady quavered out, "you put it in your own way. I mean that you 'll cool off. You already *have* —— !" And on this, the next instant, her tears began to flow. She succumbed to them and collapsed ; she sank down again, burying her face and trying to smother her sobs.

Her young friend stood there, still in some rigour, but taken much by surprise even if not yet fully moved to pity. "I don't put anything in any ' way,' and I 'm very glad you 're suited. Only, you know, you did put to me so splendidly what, even for me, if I had listened to you, it might lead to."

Mrs. Jordan kept up a mild thin weak wail ; then, drying her eyes, as feebly considered this reminder. "It has led to my not starving !" she faintly gasped.

Our young lady, at this, dropped into the place beside her, and now, in a rush, the small silly misery was clear. She took her hand as a sign of pitying it, then, after another instant, confirmed this expression with a consoling kiss. They sat there together ; they looked out, hand in hand, into the damp dusky shabby little room and into the future, of no such very different suggestion, at last accepted by each. There was no definite utterance, on either side, of Mr. Drake's position in the great world, but the temporary collapse of his prospective bride threw all further necessary light ; and what our heroine saw and felt for in the whole business was the vivid reflexion of her own dreams and delusions and her own return to reality. Reality, for the poor things they both were, could only be ugliness and obscurity, could never be the escape, the rise. She pressed her friend — she had tact enough for that — with no other personal question, brought on no need of further revelations, only just continued to hold and comfort her and to acknowledge by stiff little forbearances the common element in their fate. She felt indeed magnanimous in such matters ; since if it was very well, for condolence or reassurance, to suppress just then invidious shrinkings, she yet by no means saw herself sitting down, as she might say, to the same table with Mr. Drake. There would luckily, to all appearance, be little question of tables ; and the circumstance that, on their peculiar lines, her friend's interests would still attach themselves to Mayfair flung over Chalk Farm the first radiance it had shown. Where was one's pride and one's passion when the real way to judge of one's luck was by making not the wrong but the right comparison ? Before she had again gathered herself to go she felt very small and cautious and thankful. "We shall have our own house," she said, "and you must come very soon and let me show it you."

"*We* shall have our own too," Mrs. Jordan replied ; "for, don't you know ? he makes it a condition that he sleeps out ? "

"A condition ? " — the girl felt out of it.

"For any new position. It was on that he parted with Lord Rye. His lordship can't meet it. So Mr. Drake has given him up."

"And all for you ? " — our young woman put it as cheerfully as possible.

"For me and Lady Bradeen. Her ladyship 's too glad to get him at any price. Lord Rye, out of interest in us, has in fact quite *made* her take him. So, as I tell you, he will have his own establishment."

167

IN THE CAGE

Mrs. Jordan, in the elation of it, had begun to
revive ; but there was nevertheless between them
rather a conscious pause — a pause in which
neither visitor nor hostess brought out a hope
or an invitation. It expressed in the last resort
that, in spite of submission and sympathy, they
could now after all only look at each other
across the social gulf. They remained together
as if it would be indeed their last chance, still
sitting, though awkwardly, quite close, and feeling also — and this most unmistakeably — that
there was one thing more to go into. By the time
it came to the surface, moreover, our young friend
had recognised the whole of the main truth, from
which she even drew again a slight irritation.
It was not the main truth perhaps that most
signified ; but after her momentary effort, her
embarrassment and her tears Mrs. Jordan had
begun to sound afresh — and even without speaking — the note of a social connexion. She had n't
really let go of it that she was marrying into
society. Well, it was a harmless compensation,
and it was all the prospective bride of Mr. Mudge
had to leave with her

XXVII

THIS young lady at last rose again, but she lingered before going. "And has Captain Everard nothing to say to it?"

"To what, dear?"

"Why, to such questions — the domestic arrangements, things in the house."

"How *can* he, with any authority, when nothing in the house is his?"

"Not his?" The girl wondered, perfectly conscious of the appearance she thus conferred on Mrs. Jordan of knowing, in comparison with herself, so tremendously much about it Well, there were things she wanted so to get at that she was willing at last, though it hurt her, to pay for them with humiliation "Why are they not his?"

"Don't you know, dear, that he has nothing?"

"Nothing?" It was hard to see him in such a light, but Mrs. Jordan's power to answer for it had a superiority that began, on the spot, to grow. "Isn't he rich?"

Mrs. Jordan looked immensely, looked both

generally and particularly, informed. " It depends upon what you call —— ! Not at any rate in the least as *she* is. What does he bring ? Think what she has. And then, love, his debts."

" His debts ? " His young friend was fairly betrayed into helpless innocence. She could struggle a little, but she had to let herself go ; and if she had spoken frankly she would have said : " Do tell me, for I don't know so much about him as *that !* " As she did n't speak frankly she only said : " His debts are nothing — when she so adores him."

Mrs. Jordan began to fix her again, and now she saw that she must only take it all. That was what it had come to : his having sat with her there on the bench and under the trees in the summer darkness and put his hand on her, making her know what he would have said if permitted ; his having returned to her afterwards, repeatedly, with supplicating eyes and a fever in his blood ; and her having, on her side, hard and pedantic, helped by some miracle and with her impossible condition, only answered him, yet supplicating back, through the bars of the cage, — all simply that she might hear of him, now for ever lost, only through Mrs. Jordan, who touched him through Mr. Drake, who reached him through Lady Bradeen. " She adores him

— but of course that was n't all there was about it."

The girl met her eyes a minute, then quite surrendered. "What was there else about it?"

"Why, don't you know?" — Mrs. Jordan was almost compassionate.

Her interlocutress had, in the cage, sounded depths, but there was a suggestion here somehow of an abyss quite measureless. "Of course I know she would never let him alone."

"How *could* she — fancy! — when he had so compromised her?"

The most artless cry they had ever uttered broke, at this, from the younger pair of lips. "*Had* he so ——?"

"Why, don't you know the scandal?"

Our heroine thought, recollected; there was something, whatever it was, that she knew after all much more of than Mrs. Jordan. She saw him again as she had seen him come that morning to recover the telegram — she saw him as she had seen him leave the shop. She perched herself a moment on this. "Oh there was nothing public."

"Not exactly public — no. But there was an awful scare and an awful row. It was all on the very point of coming out Something was lost — something was found."

" Ah yes," the girl replied, smiling as if with the revival of a blurred memory ; " something was found."

" It all got about — and there was a point at which Lord Bradeen had to act."

" Had to — yes   But he did n't."

Mrs. Jordan was obliged to admit it. " No, he did n't.   And then, luckily for them, he died."

" I did n't know about his death," her companion said.

" It was nine weeks ago, and most sudden.   It has given them a prompt chance."

" To get married " — this was a wonder — " within nine weeks ? "

" Oh not immediately, but — in all the circumstances — very quietly and, I assure you, very soon.   Every preparation 's made.   Above all she holds him."

" Oh yes, she holds him ! " our young friend threw off.   She had this before her again a minute ;   then she continued :   " You mean through his having made her talked about ? "

" Yes, but not only that.   She has still another pull."

" Another ? "

Mrs. Jordan hesitated.   " Why, he was *in* something."

Her comrade wondered.   " In what ? "

172

"I don't know. Something bad. As I tell you, something was found."

The girl stared. "Well?"

"It would have been very bad for him. But she helped him some way — she recovered it, got hold of it. It's even said she stole it!"

Our young woman considered afresh. "Why it was what was found that precisely saved him."

Mrs. Jordan, however, was positive. "I beg your pardon. I happen to know."

Her disciple faltered but an instant. "Do you mean through Mr. Drake? Do they tell *him* these things?"

"A good servant," said Mrs. Jordan, now thoroughly superior and proportionately senten-tious, "does n't need to be told! Her ladyship saved — as a woman so often saves! — the man she loves."

This time our heroine took longer to recover herself, but she found a voice at last. "Ah well — of course I don't know! The great thing was that he got off. They seem then, in a manner," she added, "to have done a great deal for each other."

"Well, it's she that has done most. She has him tight."

"I see, I see. Good-bye." The women had already embraced, and this was not repeated;
173

but Mrs. Jordan went down with her guest to the door of the house. Here again the younger lingered, reverting, though three or four other remarks had on the way passed between them, to Captain Everard and Lady Bradeen. "Did you mean just now that if she had n't saved him, as you call it, she would n't hold him so tight?"

"Well, I dare say." Mrs. Jordan, on the door-step, smiled with a reflexion that had come to her; she took one of her big bites of the brown gloom. "Men always dislike one when they 've done one an injury."

"But what injury had he done her?"

"The one I 've mentioned. He *must* marry her, you know."

"And did n't he want to?"

"Not before."

"Not before she recovered the telegram?"

Mrs. Jordan was pulled up a little. "Was it a telegram?"

The girl hesitated. "I thought you said so. I mean whatever it was."

"Yes, whatever it was, I don't think she saw *that.*"

"So she just nailed him?"

"She just nailed him." The departing friend was now at the bottom of the little flight of steps; the other was at the top, with a certain
174

thickness of fog. "And when am I to think of you in your little home ? — next month ? " asked the voice from the top.

" At the very latest   And when am I to think of you in yours ? "

" Oh even sooner. I feel, after so much talk with you about it, as if I were already there ! " Then " *Good*-bye ! " came out of the fog.

" Good-*bye !* " went into it.   Our young lady went into it also, in the opposed quarter, and presently, after a few sightless turns, came out on the Paddington canal.   Distinguishing vaguely what the low parapet enclosed she stopped close to it and stood a while very intently, but perhaps still sightlessly, looking down on it. A policeman, while she remained, strolled past her ; then, going his way a little further and half lost in the atmosphere, paused and watched her.   But she was quite unaware — she was full of her thoughts. They were too numerous to find a place just here, but two of the number may at least be mentioned. One of these was that, decidedly, her little home must be not for next month, but for next week ; the other, which came indeed as she resumed her walk and went her way, was that it was strange such a matter should be at last settled for her by Mr. Drake

PRINTED BY
WILLIAM BRENDON AND SON, LTD.
PLYMOUTH ENGLAND